THE BODY AUCTION

THE BODY AUCTION

LAYLA MATTHEWS

Palmetto Publishing Group
Charleston, SC

The Body Auction
Copyright © 2018 by Layla Matthews
All rights reserved

This is a work of fiction. Names, characters, places, and incidents either are the products of the author's imagination or are used fictitiously. Any resemblance to actual persons, living or dead, businesses, companies, events, or locales is entirely coincidental.

First Edition
Cover by Deborah Stikes " The Portrait House"
Printed in the United States

ISBN-13: 978-1-64111-152-2
ISBN-10: 1-64111-152-6

PROLOGUE

rchids. No, tulips. Maybe roses—yes, definitely roses. The smell is overwhelming and very obnoxious. Nausea pours over me in strong waves; I feel my stomach muscles contract in spams. The feeling of weakness is profound, and my legs and arms feel like thousands of pins and needles are sticking in them. They are numb and weak all at the same time. My eyelids will not open, and panic is setting in. I have no idea what has happened.

Every fiber in my body is on edge. I cannot move, cannot open my eyes, but I can feel every inch of my skin. Why can I not move my body? My arms are laid by my side, bent at the elbows and hands across my chest. I am trying to wake up, trying to make myself wake up. This feels like a horrible nightmare, the type I have when I've taken cold medication. But I don't remember taking cold medicine. I can feel my heart racing; it sounds like a sledgehammer in my chest. But my breathing feels so odd, so slow.

I am an educated woman; I know I need to think rational-
ly and calm down. I have been a nurse long enough to know
something is wrong with my body. Maybe I've been in a car
accident, or I may be dead. No, that's crazy, I'm not dead.

I hear a sound that sends chills down my spine, the type
you have when fingernails go down a chalkboard. I hear my
husband, Tripp, crying. He is very near where my head is lying.
He is sobbing, talking to me, saying how much he loves me,
needs me. Sounds of others talking and weeping can be heard
faintly in the background. Sadness and fear overcome me. Slow,
sad music is barely audible. This feels so familiar; this must be
a dream I've had before. But the next noise should have awakened me. I hear my daughter, Aubrey, screaming, crying as I
have never heard in all her twenty-one years. Then a horrible
realization happens: I am in a funeral home, in the casket. I
have been the mourner—now I am the one being mourned.

I feel utter terror rage through every cell in my body. They
think I'm dead . . . am I? I try to move, try to scream, but nothing. My body feels like it is asleep, but all my nerve endings
are firing at top speed. As my mind races on the possibilities of
how this could have happened, I must pass out. This repeats
over and over for what seems like hours; people come and go.
Some voices I recognize; some I do not. My eyes refuse to
open. I cannot move any part of my body at all. Then a shroud
of silence, and that is the end of the first night that will forever
change my life as I know it.

CHAPTER 1

That night changed my and my family's lives in a way that seemed incomprehensible. This is where my story begins.

My name is Layla Matthews. I am a nurse practitioner and have been for fifteen years. I have a wonderful husband named Tripp and a daughter in college, Aubrey. We live in a small town in North Carolina, the Bible Belt. Raised by a Baptist minister and in a very strict, conservative home, I had a great faith and an essentially good life. I knew to respect my elders, not to cuss, not to drink, and that the ten commandments were the rules we lived our lives by. So, you see, this is why, while I was lying there, that night, I questioned everything I had ever heard on Sunday mornings. I was not in Heaven, I didn't think this was Hell, but it may have been. So, let me tell you about the night I died.

I was an intensive care nurse for many years. I never liked taking care of the patients on life support that we had to use paralytics on. These are medications given intravenously that paralyze your body. They were used only in very critically ill patients who needed special ventilation, when the body needed to be completely still. But the issue with those patients was that you had to be sure they had other medications to adequately sedate them so they were not "awake" and paralyzed. In the case that the patient was not sedated enough, they would be able to hear and feel everything. This would be torture for this person. That night, I knew just how those patients must have felt.

After all the noise stopped that night and I was alone, I did panic for what seemed like hours. I questioned my faith, God, and all that I knew to be true, fact, and concrete. When I could calm myself, I realized I was not dead. I refused to believe this was it, this was the end! I decided to use my brain and analyze what I knew around me. Something had happened to make people believe I was dead. How was this even possible currently in modern medicine? I could hear, I could smell, and as time passed, I started to have different sensations in my body.

So, I knew where I was: a casket in a funeral home. I tried to think back to the last thing I could remember. I tried to focus and calm myself. Slowly, my mind cleared, and the fog lifted. I had worked for the hospitalist the night before. I did this sometimes to moonlight. It was good money and easy work. The night had been slow, only five admissions from the ER, but since I had worked the day before at the office, I was exhausted. So, as always, I would go to the on-call room to try to sleep a little in between admissions. I hated that room. It was in the back of the hospital, the old part. It was dark and creepy, and it was closed to patients. I always heard noises and felt on edge when I was out there in the middle of the night. But none of that was new, nothing out of the ordinary. Thinking back to my very last memory, I could remember . . . nothing, absolutely nothing.

I would cry, but there were no sounds, no tears. The frigid air shrouded around me like a dark cloak. My arms by my side, close, very close. The sides of the box seemed to be caving in around me, and the panic inside me started to once again arise, erupting through me like a volcano. The fabric touching my skin was soft and cool, satin. Sleep came and went, alternating between terror and calm. Then, finally, I awoke to a new sensation . . . pain! I welcomed it, I delighted in it. I could *feel* something. My back was throbbing; the coffin was hard and like lying on a cement slab. If I could have only moved, repositioned, but I couldn't, no matter how hard I tried. I guessed no one ever worried about the comfort of a coffin. I mean, you were dead. Who cared if the place you are lying on was hard?

The next thing that happened was the turning point for me in this nightmare. I heard more voices, not sad ones. They sounded happy and excited. I could not recognize who they were. Then a loud scraping sound, and I felt my coffin move. Someone was moving it very slightly. A pulling sensation at my left groin, a pinch and a burning. That was the moment I realized I had some type of intravenous line in my groin. Whoever the men were, I could deduce, were putting medication into the line. Don't get me wrong—I was terrified, but also slightly relieved. I was not dead, and I had an idea what was happening to me. But something had gone wrong, I felt a cold liquid drip down my left buttock and thigh. It felt wet and cool. I strained my ears to try to make out what they were talking about. Two men, laughing and joking. One voice so familiar, yet they sounded so distant. When my coffin was moved back to the original position, I could make out what they were saying more clearly. They were meeting someone, lots of numbers, money, and they were listing women's names. Cold wetness engulfed my once numb buttock. I could feel the liquid; it was miserable and amazing at the same time. Each moment that passed, I seem to have increased sensations in my body. A tingle here and a little pain there. My mind was searching and rationalizing what was going on. It was obvious I had been given a drug that would make me appear dead; I could only have enough muscle function to have shallow respirations but not move any other muscles. The question I replayed over and over was why? Who would do this and why? What kind of sick psychopath could ever even conceive of something like this?

After I had fallen asleep, more noises awakened me. Music. The soft, sad music was playing again. But it seemed different; more light was permeating into my previously dark box. Like when you wake up in the morning and the sun is coming into the window, it is bright even before you open your eyes. That's how it seemed to me. I felt extremely wet now. The medication had leaked down to my lower back and to my knee. It was like how it felt to wear a wet bathing suit home from the beach, miserable and cold. It was quite clear that the intravenous line had come loose, unhooked, or malfunctioned. Waves of nausea were the next thing to assault me. The smells of those roses were so pungent now. It burned my nose, and it seemed like they were blowing rose fumes straight into the casket. Another form of torture, I assumed. As the nausea progressed, I gagged, and as sick as I felt, excitement surged through me as I noticed my tongue move!

I could hear the pastor talk about my life, offer words of comfort for my grieving family. He offered them peace that I was in Heaven. Next, a choir sang; I made a mental note to discuss the horrible song choices with my family when I got out of this nightmare. Loud cries—I could hear sobbing from someone. My chest hurt and filled with emotion for the person who was so distraught. They didn't know I was in there. I wanted to scream, yell, comfort them, but I could not. Even though my tongue could move, I still could not open my lips.

Knowing what came next, after the funeral, the emotion that had become too real to me reared its head again: terror! I would be buried alive soon. I lay there, and I prayed.

Focusing all my attention on my body, I tried to move a digit at a time, twitch a muscle, something. Finally, after channeling all my energy, my big toe on my left foot moved, my right pinky, left thigh, and right shoulder. Suddenly, my left leg jumped, hard. Did the casket move? It had to because that was a hard spasm, but no one came, no sounds, no screams. My time was running out, and I prayed for something to happen, anything to happen.

CHAPTER 2

Darkness, movement. The casket was closed, and I was in the hearse, moving. Despite trying everything I could, I could not move enough to be noticed. Miserable could not begin to describe how I felt. As the medication effects were wearing off, every nerve ending and muscle seemed to be revolting against me. I felt like one hundred hornets were in the box, stinging me all at the same time. This dress was too tight; the wet satin was making me feel damp and cold. But what was awaiting me would be even worse than this. I would be buried alive and feel myself die slowly.

Then the good Lord must have heard my plea because the last piece of tape came loose. Thank goodness for curvy country roads. The previous curve was so sharp the casket moved, and that's when the last strip could not hold its grip any longer. Fluids poured into my already wet groin like a faucet had been turned on. That was what was good about these types of medications; they had a very short half-life, meaning they wore off quickly. By the time the car was parked, my whole body was exploding from the inside out.

The knocking was what did it—the knocking with my right hand on the coffin. When Aubrey came up to the casket to lay the proverbial last rose, grief overwhelmed her. She threw her body over the top; she was weeping, overcome with the thought of telling me a final goodbye. As bad as I hated to do it, to traumatize her, I had to do something. The scream that resounded from my daughter could have won a Grammy. She would have made any horror movie proud with the high-pitched shriek she produced. Of course, commotion ensued after this display. Tripp's voice was next, trying to comfort his baby girl. He begged and pleaded with her, trying to move her off the top of my coffin. But I had to admire my hard-headed daughter; she was sure she had heard something and had a death grip on the handles of my box of death. I was trying to knock again and again, but with the other hysteria, it was not heard. Finally, when things calmed down, Tripp's voice low, whispering and trying to reason with her, one last knock did it.

Brief silence then all pandemonium broke loose. Yelling and screaming, he had heard me. My husband's voice boomed orders to the funeral directors. He demanded the coffin be opened, and the funeral directors explained to him that once sealed, it cannot be reopened. After what seemed like hours, his persistence paid off. They got the lid open; the light was so bright it hurt my eyes. The heat on my skin was immediate and so warm. I felt like it had been years since I'd felt the warmth of the sun. I still could not open my eyes, but only one movement, and Tripp wrapped his strong arms around me and lifted me up out of the box that had held me captive. I don't remember what felt the best at that moment: the fact I was rescued or the feeling of my husband's arms around me. My nightmare was over at last! Or at least that's what I thought.

CHAPTER 3

Being at the same job and working at the same hospital for fifteen years gave me the blessing of a large group of friends who were there that day. Some were in shock; some passed out. My parents were also standing in utter terror. Really, in this day in time, how many people do you see literally "rise from death"? Paramedics arrived, police, and the scene quickly went crazier than you can imagine. Finally, in the ER, my mouth was released, and then after more tedious work, my eyes. The lights were unbearable; I had been in the dark for so long. But seeing my family, hearing them, and touching them was the best feeling in the world. No time was wasted, and question after question was thrown at me. I had no answers, no idea how this happened.

My rescue came when the physician in charge of my care put his foot down and made the police and other family leave. Tripp and Aubrey could stay, my saviors. For the first few moments alone, we just held one another and cried. Emotions ran over all of us—mine, relief, and theirs, relief, but of a different kind. Finally, Dr. Ricardo asked for a few moments alone. He was a friend to me; I had worked with him for many years. A brilliant physician, caring and funny. We both had crazy personalities, so when we had the same schedule, we always liked to talk and hang out. He had been at the funeral that day, and he had not left my side. He examined me, and this was the first time I could assess the damage for myself. I was pale, thin, and had a large hematoma (bruise) all down my left thigh, starting at my groin. My muscles had wasted away, and my skin was thin and frail. Odd bruising all over my body was noted. Labs were done, hair samples taken. My extremities felt like Jell-O. After multiple CAT scans, labs, and an exam, we tried to talk while awaiting the results.

News of this magnitude had spread like wildfire. Soon, the small, rural hospital was swarmed with news vans, reporters, and police. Questions, assumptions, blame were going in all directions. I lay there in the bed, weak, clueless, happy to be out of my box. No satin sheets for the rest of my life, and I did not care to ever smell the putrid aroma of a rose again. A plethora of visitors came by, limited to only immediate family and closest friends. Tears of joy over and over, the same comments: "How could this happen?" "Are you going to sue the funeral home?" It felt like the same record was being played over and over. By the time night came, I was exhausted. Tripp and Aubrey slept that night with me, in the hospital bed, lights on, cotton sheets. Strict instructions were sent out: NO roses!

Three days passed before the real investigation began. The police and FBI had been trying to gather what they could, but the key piece of the puzzle was me, and I just could not wrap my mind around what had happened. I would awaken and feel like this had all been a very weird dream. A police detective named Jimmy Whiteside came to see me daily. He was Southern and charming, not pushy but clearly wanted answers. Answers I could not give. Over and over, we replayed that night. According to Tripp, I had texted him that I was leaving that morning as I always did but never returned home.

My car had been found off an embankment. My family had been informed that I had fallen asleep and died at the scene of massive internal injuries. They pronounced me dead at the scene, and I was never taken to the ER—straight to the funeral home. But what was so strange was I could not remember getting into my car at all. The last thing I could recall was going back to the call room to lie down; I didn't remember even texting my husband.

Day after day, I became stronger. Paralytics were not used often due to the severe muscle damage they can cause, and I could see why. Learning to walk all over again at the age of forty was rough, to say the least. My legs had lost all muscle tone. They were thin and pale, and just to stand was a huge effort. It felt like when you are a child and are trying to learn how to ride a bike. Fellow nurses, doctors, and friends came by often. Aubrey stayed by my side at all times. After two weeks, Tripp had went back to work. All my testing was normal, except I had been intentionally sedated and made to look dead, and the reason was still a mystery. One odd thing did become apparent; I had undergone a liver biopsy, a heart catherization, and a kidney biopsy. This was what the odd bruising was from.

Detective Whiteside kept me up to date on the investigation. The funeral home was immediately closed, and the FBI was looking for answers. They felt like this was where the problem was until one day, I was outside in the hallway, and all of that changed with one word. Due to the severe muscle wasting in my legs, I had to work with physical therapy daily. Some great friends work in that department and always worked so hard to help me. They pushed me to my limits and cheered me up. Some of the highlights of my day was to get up and try to recover, walk, and get stronger. But the fatigue was overwhelming. My muscles would shake and tremor in revolt. Sleep was hard for me; the nightmares were horrible. Aubrey slept with me, but I still awoke in terror. Of course, they had the psychiatrist come see me. I was given antidepressants and anti-anxiety pills, but I refused. I was never a fan of taking medications before, and now it was worse. I was determined to deal with it my way, on my own.

This specific day, I was out in the hall working on climbing steps when I heard *his* voice. I froze; urine leaked from my bladder before I had any warning to control it. The severe trembling came next; sweat poured from my forehead. Sara in PT was asking me something, if I was okay, but I could not answer. I could hear her voice, but it was like she was in a tunnel far away. I just stood there. Aubrey was yelling my name; they were reassuring her that I had just overworked myself and was weak. But she knew—she knows me better than anyone, and she knew something else was wrong.

Dr. Ricardo had remained my attending physician and came by daily even when he was off. He was on the fifth floor that day and came over when he heard the commotion. As he assisted getting me back to my room, I looked around at the faces. Staring at me, whispers. New nurses who didn't know me were awkward; old ones had looks of concern and pity. As we walked around the corner of the desk, I could see into the small dictation room where physicians dictated notes and consults. That was when I saw him, and I knew what voice I had heard that night in my box of death.

Dr. Michael Pierce had been with the hospitalist program for only about six months. He was a young doctor, cocky and rude. Thought he was brilliant but was an idiot. He was certain he was God's gift to the young pretty nurses, and he did manage to seduce many of them. He was the type of new physician all seasoned nurses hated. Condescending, never taking a recommendation even if the nurse was correct. He would let a patient die before he would admit he was wrong. He was a man, he had MD by his name, and in his tiny man brain, he was a *god*. I had a few issues with him over some patient care, but I was old and experienced and was not intimidated at all. But on that day, he terrified me because I knew that voice. I knew that was the voice I had heard and recognized that night. At that moment, I remembered something: I had seen him the night I was working. I wondered why he was there so late and even enquired about it, but he said he was just catching up on some dictations. I really didn't give it another thought until then.

Dr. Ricardo had my left arm, Sara my right, and they both felt the tension surge once again throughout my body. Fear ripped to my very core. That was that last thing I remembered before I passed out.

Tripp was at my bedside when I woke up. He looked so worried. My handsome husband looked exhausted, and this ordeal had aged him ten years. Aubrey had called him, and he had immediately come. Dr. Ricardo assured them it was anxiety and exhaustion and it would pass. But Aubrey knew; she knew something had happened, and so did Sara. Detective Whiteside had made his visit right after I had passed out, but Aubrey had let him know that something just wasn't right. He was soon by my bed when I was up and talking. I asked everyone to step out but him. I told him what I remembered and about the voice and seeing Dr. Pierce that night. He listened, took notes, had a perplexed expression, and then left abruptly. I was a little hurt. Was I insane? Did he think I was having side effects from the trauma? That night, the nightmares were the worst. Sleep would never be the same for me.

CHAPTER 4

That same week, I was moved to the first-floor skilled unit for more rehab. I didn't hear from Detective Whiteside for two days but did notice some differences, subtle as they were. I had limited visitors, a guard was outside my door all the time, and I was told to keep what I heard and saw to myself and tell no one else. The day the detective came by, I was excited to listen to what developments had taken place. He had left in a hurry because he had remembered something odd about the accident report. A physician had been one of the first on the scene; he pronounced me dead, informed the first responders, and called the coroner. When the paramedics arrived, he refused to let them near me. They put this in the police report, and no one had looked into it even though it was quite odd and didn't follow proper protocol. He had questioned the paramedic at the scene, who had been very upset and did not agree with how it was handled. (But by then, the police were there, and felt it was okay to bypass the hospital. After all, I was already dead; what good would it do?) And guess who the physician was? The one and only Dr. Pierce. He had used the name of another physician, but when the paramedics and first responders were shown a picture, they verified who it was.

I wasn't crazy; it had been his voice that night, and he was there at my crash scene. Questions were pouring from me, but Detective Whiteside just sat there and shook his head. I was like a four-year-old; I shot question after question at the detective. He did not know what was going on, but he wanted to wait to do anything. I was safe, no one could hurt me here, and I was to trust no one. He warned me not to tell anyone of these developments, not even Dr. Ricardo. My mind was flying. I asked myself, *Is he insane?* Did he think my coworkers and friends had anything to do with this? I lay there furious, hurt, and confused.

That night, while Aubrey slept in her bed pulled up beside mine, I saw my phone light up. I quietly peeked at it and saw a new Snapchat. From Sara, which was odd, especially in the middle of the night, so, of course, I opened it. The thing about a "snap" is that when it disappears, it is gone, but what I saw in those ten seconds sent a chill to my bones. She said, "You are not safe here. Get out. Hurry!" Then, as quickly as it had come, it was gone.

Sara Mathis was a young, beautiful physical therapist. She was married to a respiratory therapist and loved her job. They had not been married long, and when they worked the same shift, they would sometimes hook up in the stairwell. No one knew but her close friends because, of course, they would be fired. But I loved her and thought it was romantic and sweet.

She always made me laugh, and I never saw her sad or act harshly with my patients, no matter how difficult they could be. She was always laughing and joking, one of those people who never had a serious moment.

After that obscure Snapchat, I asked my nurse to have Sara help me out of bed.

Aubrey ran home to shower, so I had a chance to talk to her alone. She walked in the door, pale and anxious. I had never seen her this way. She wouldn't say anything in front of my nurse and quickly made an excuse for me to take a shower. I was embarrassed. Did I smell? Lying in a hospital bed doesn't allow you to be the freshest, but I did try to sponge off daily. After her persistence, she told the CNA (nursing assistant) that she would help me and do my exercises.

Once in the bathroom, with the shower running, she leaned in and whispered in my ear. Then I knew what she was doing—trying to make sure no one heard what she had to tell me. She had been in the stairwell having a little rendezvous when the door on the upper level opened. Her husband was able to get out quietly, but Sara was stuck hiding behind some boxes. This was not a big deal; they liked the excitement of almost getting caught. It happened all the time, but this time she heard something. It was a man she did not recognize and Dr. Pierce. The strange man was furious, and he kept asking over and over how a mistake of this magnitude had happened. Dr. Pierce explained that "the line must have become loose" and I had not gotten enough of the medication to keep me sedated. When it finally completely unhooked, I was able to move. The arguing had been intense, and while Sara was talking, I became dizzy. She said the man threatened Dr. Pierce. The man was reassured when he let him know that he had been reviewing my chart and they were worried that I had severe PTSD (post-traumatic stress disorder.) He was planning to "take care of me" and make it look like I overdosed. They could not be sure what I had heard or could remember. My mind was reeling with questions. Why would they want to kill me?

Sara quickly helped me redress and again expressed her concern for me. I explained to her not to tell a person; I was worried for her safety. She agreed and left me, alone and wondering what to do next. Requesting a laptop was the top of my priority list. But not a hospital-issued one, so I had Aubrey bring hers to me. I started researching Dr. Pierce, quickly discovering that hospitals do not screen physicians closely enough. He was virtually unknown until five years ago. No records anywhere—very odd, I thought.

Then Det. Whiteside arrived. I needed to tell him what had happened, but I couldn't take him in the shower with me. I requested assistance and asked to go outside. It had been so long since I had been out in the open air; it felt so good. When the detective pushed the wheelchair out the doors, the warm breeze hit my face. The sun was so bright; I was having a tough time adjusting my eyes. The air was so refreshing. I had no idea how good it would feel. I felt almost normal, free in some ways. The world was out there, big and beautiful. I wanted to get up and run, run far away and forget this nightmare ever happened to me. But instead, I explained everything to him. He agreed that this doctor was not who he said he was. He had found this man using multiple aliases all over the US and Europe.

While he sat and filled me in, a tall man walked up and sat down. I was horrified when the detective kept talking so openly. Then he decided to introduce us; this new mystery man was named Steven Johnson, FBI. He was handsome, dark, and seemed serious. He made me nervous and very self-aware of my probable horrific appearance. I had not cared what I looked like; I was depressed and overwhelmed. But in his presence, I was embarrassed to look disheveled. Mr. Johnson did not interject for a while, and the detective kept updating me. Then he spoke up and explained he was with the FBI and would be assisting with my case. He was blunt and rude. No compassion for the horrible ordeal I had gone through. He basically told me to get over it, be the strong woman he knew I could be, and help them get to the bottom of this.

Furious was not the word to describe me. How dare this man I didn't even know come in here and lecture me? I could still barely move my extremities, I'd almost been buried alive, I could not sleep, and I did not need his attitude. I refused to speak with him and was taken back to my room. He followed us in the hospital, and when getting on the elevator, Dr. Ricardo got in. When he enquired about who I was with, Mr. Johnson spoke up and told him he was my cousin who had come in from Kentucky to see me. I played along and never blinked an eye.

The events that happened over the next few weeks seemed like they happened in a whirlwind. The detective and Agent

Johnson had gone to my home and met with Tripp and Aubrey. They were updated, and the details I had been told to keep secret were finally divulged to them. A computer specialist from the FBI was tracking the activity in my electronic medical record and could see how often Dr. Pierce accessed it.

Early one morning, Dr. Narran came to see me. He was the psychiatrist who had come by on many occasions. He was friendly but wasn't pleased that I had refused the medications he wanted me to take. However, I had been instructed to agree this time. Soon, Haldol, Ativan, and Cymbalta were added to my med list. Anti-anxiety, anti-depressives were going to help me sleep and help my PTSD. The detectives wanted it to be very apparent that I had agreed and was going to take the medications. Being drug-naïve, I never could have taken these medications and not been in a drugged stupor. So, when the nurse brought them to me, on a scheduled basis, either Aubrey or Tripp would make some small distraction to give me a chance to hide them somewhere in my bed or chair. I hated the fact that my family was involved in this, but the more information we obtained, the more disturbing the case became.

The plan was to let Dr. Pierce make his move. I secretly worked with Sara when no one was looking. I got stronger and more determined every day. My depression and anxiety turned to anger and rage.

The first encounter with Agent Johnson had been strained at best, but as the weeks passed, we got closer. He was a serious man who had served in Desert Storm Special Forces. Due to his incredible skills, he'd been asked to join the FBI. He had skills that no one had and contacts that the FBI didn't even know about.

The only people who knew what was going on were the detective, Agent Johnson, Sara, and my husband and daughter. At first, the fear overpowered me, Sara, and my family. But soon, we wanted answers and worked secretly with the FBI. We had no idea who we could trust, so we told no one. When the nurses did their assessments, I faked weakness, lay in the bed, and appeared depressed. I think I should have been an actress; my skills were quite exceptional. Aubrey played it up also. She even cried one day when I refused to get out of bed for the nurse and ran from the room dramatically. I almost laughed at her emotional display. But it worked like a charm; they charted day after day how lethargic, depressed, and unwilling to participate I was. Sara made sure she documented how weak I was, how I could not stand up without two people to assist. I felt terrible for Dr. Ricardo; he tried day after day to reason with me. He tried every technique he could to motivate me, but nothing worked. I wanted to tell him the truth but was quickly reminded that the players in the sick, twisted game were not known.

It seemed as if we were at a standstill. I wanted to get this over with and have answers, but the detectives are slow and calculated. They knew much more information than we did, and I was getting restless and impatient. Those four walls and bed were starting to drive me insane.

The next day, I knew by the look on Agent Johnson's face that something had changed. He was serious, strained, and barely spoke at all until he had rolled me outside to talk. He was impatient with me while I acted all pathetic getting out of bed, not like usual. His news was disturbing. Dr. Pierce had been accessing my record much more frequently. They felt we were running out of time. The goal was to find out the why since they knew the who. He informed me that my medication regimen had been adjusted early that morning. My typical pills had stayed the same, but now an IV sedative had been ordered at bedtime. I felt myself start to panic because I could fake taking the pills, but what could I do about an IV medication? Agent Johnson saw my worry and reassured me that he had everything under control.

As he rolled me back to my room, we saw Dr. Ricardo and Dr. Pierce in the hallway. Like nothing out of the ordinary, Dr. Ricardo stopped us and tried to have a conversation. I tried not to have a full-blown panic attack and was proud of myself when I was able to speak and be as normal as possible. But I was wondering the whole time, what kind of sick psychopath was standing before me? In his starched white lab coat, Littman stethoscope around his neck, Mont Blanc pen in his pocket, he looked like an ordinary physician. It was no different than a Halloween costume to me because he was no healer! This was a monster, and for some unknown reason, this monster had picked me as his victim.

That night, my fear came true. There was nothing I could do about the IV Valium that the nurse put into my IV line. I tried to refuse but was quickly dismissed. I slept like a rock all night and half the rest of the day. I was scared that I may not wake up, but thank God, I did. That brain fog and the lethargic feeling lasted up until that night.

That afternoon, when Dr. Ricardo made rounds, I asked why the medication had been added, and he expressed his concern about my night terrors. But I had not discussed this with him, and I was shocked by his statement. This was the first sign that Dr. Pierce was not doing this alone. They had been correct to have me trust no one. I was sure I had not told anyone about the horrible dreams that haunted me, so why would he assume that? I was sad and felt betrayed. I had considered Dr. Ricardo my friend. He was so handsome and charismatic. He had a personality that made you enjoy just sitting next to him at the desk. Honestly, had I been single, I would have been interested in him romantically. But this didn't mean he was involved. The nurses may have reported my lack of sleep, but I would continue to be cautious, as I had been directed.

CHAPTER 5

Due to hospitals' poor treatment of nurses, patient load, and poor benefits, many experienced nurses retired early or simply resigned. So that night, I was not shocked to have a new RN. She was a travel nurse. This meant she was not an employee of the hospital, but they paid an agency for them to come for a certain period. She was in her thirties, dark-headed, and very efficient. She was also drop-dead gorgeous! Her hair was black and long, and her body was perfect. She did not speak a lot and at times seemed almost harsh. I had continued to work with Sara daily and was amazingly stronger. I could walk steps, lift weights, and was in better shape than I had ever been. If I wasn't an amazing actress, I felt sure I would have been discharged home by now.

My new nurse, Kayleigh, was not very friendly to Sara; she was quite rude. She was kicked out of my room and was not allowed to help me back into bed. I was thinking maybe she was working with Dr. Pierce, and I was trying to get a message to the agent somehow when it was time for my nightly meds. I was terrified when she came in. I was sure this was it and she was going to overdose me. She had the syringe in her hand picked up my IV, but instead of putting the needle in the port, she placed it right beside of it, squirting the medication into the sheets. Aubrey and I both saw what had taken place. My mouth fell open, and when I looked up at her, she winked. That moment I knew—she was with us! Kayleigh Harris was an FBI agent that had also been trained as a nurse. She was amazing, and I instantly admired her.

Night after night, this act was repeated. Finally, I was informed that this special agent had been sent here to help me stay safe and uncover what was going on. Since she worked the night shift and there were few nurses on this shift, she would sneak me down the stairs and let me walk outside or go work out. I was smaller than I had ever been, and since I had no junk food and had to pretend to have no appetite, I continued to get in better shape and keep my weight down.

We all knew my time was running out and Pierce was going to act soon. His behavior was erratic, and they caught him on camera in a heated argument while on his cell.

I had loved getting close to Kayleigh; she was funny, smart, and very supportive. She helped me overcome my fear, never judging, and offered no pity; instead, she made me strong enough to deal with the nightmare I was in.

Then, one night, it all paid off. Since my new nurse was there five nights a week, Tripp and Aubrey went home those nights because they knew I was safe. Kayleigh would take me to the PT room, and she would often look around the hospital.

She would see how the night shift worked, who was there, who could access certain parts of the hospital. Then she would come and get me. We did the same night after night. Often, Sara would stay late and talk to me and help me. But one night, this all changed.

CHAPTER 6

The night started like any other. I had my FBI nurse, Sara was on second shift, and Tripp and Aubrey had left. I loved these nights because it was a nice break. Kayleigh came in and let me know she had seen Dr. Pierce arrive for a night shift. This would be the first time that had happened since the night I had "died." I hoped he was just covering, but I had a weird feeling something was wrong. Sara texted me and said she was going to grab a snack around 11:00 p.m. and she would be down. I had already "taken my meds," and if you had asked any of the other staff, they would have told you I was sleeping.

By 11:30 p.m., no Sara, and Kayleigh was extremely anxious to go find out what Pierce was up to. She took me down to the PT room and about drove me crazy pacing the floor. Sara was a talker and was probably gossiping somewhere, so I told her to go, that I was fine because I knew Sara would be there any moment. I guess I lost track of time because after running on the treadmill and using the rowing machine,

I could not believe it was midnight. Where was Sara? This was not like her at all. *What should I do?* I could go up alone, but the other nurses may suspect something. When Kayleigh came in, the look on her face was serious, concerned; all FBI now, my nurse was gone. She informed me that Sara had acute appendicitis and had been taken to the OR. I interrupted and let her know that I had just heard from her at 11:00 p.m.—that was impossible. The story she heard was that she had been in pain when she came into work. She complained to a physician on the floor and was quickly and discreetly evaluated as a professional courtesy of the hospital. When they felt she needed surgery, no time was wasted, and she was treated quickly.

My mind flew. I knew hospital procedure, and I knew who worked at night and how long it took a surgeon on call to get there. Something was terribly wrong. I called her husband, and he explained he had been called by a physician that he wasn't familiar with and informed that Sara was very ill and had been taken emergently to the operating room. They would not even wait for him to arrive and see her before going in. My mind was racing along with my heart. The dizziness came, and nausea and sweats came soon after. Kayleigh was in the corner on the phone with Agent Johnson. He was having the FBI look at the records as they spoke, but something wasn't making sense at all.

There had been renovations at the hospital over the years. Having worked at the hospital for so long, I knew the back stairwells, supply rooms, and secret places most people didn't know existed. The new physical therapy department was right under the operating room suites. I had to know who was doing surgery and make sure Pierce had nothing to do with it. When Kaleigh hung up, I explained that we could peek and see if this was legit. Maybe she did have a bad appendix, and we were being paranoid. She disagreed at first and insisted on taking me back to my room. But I reminded her that I was fine—the frail, weak façade was just that, an act. Sara was my friend, and I had to know she was okay. I had an odd feeling inside of me, one of impending doom I could not ignore.

We moved quietly and slowly along the dark, dusty corridor. It had been sealed off years ago. A small area of sheetrock had covered an old hallway that I remembered was there. It took some time, but we made a small enough area to crawl into. After a few minutes, we had reached one of the outside walls into the OR. The only way we could see in was through a small vent in the corner. But luckily, due to the stainless steel and flooring, the voices carried well. I did not recognize the man dressed as the surgeon. Panic swept over me; I knew all the surgeons. In a large hospital, maybe not, but in a small rural area, everyone knew the surgeons. This man was a stranger. I recognized the anesthesiologist and the scrub nurse, and then as fear and panic began to overcome me, I saw Dr. Pierce. The moment I recognized him, I started to shake. Kayleigh gave me a look of death, and I worked hard to calm myself. There are no circumstances in which a hospitalist would *ever* be in the OR, and we both knew this.

But who we saw was not the most terrifying; it was what we heard. The men were talking about me. The surgeon was yelling at Pierce about having to come clean up this mess and get a "new girl." I had never seen Pierce look so scared. Sweat beaded on his forehead. I tried to listen to them and see what I could, but our line of sight was limited. Only a split second was needed for me to see that Sara was not having surgery. They were doing a heart catheterization, and then she had a liver biopsy. The same procedures that had been performed on me! And then I saw a central line in her left groin, and I knew they were doing to Sara what they had done to me. The staging was different, but the plan was the same. What in God's name were these men doing? Names and dates were exchanged, discussions about other men and other "candidates." It was apparent that all the men in the room were taking part in this plan, whatever it was.

I had not looked over at Kayleigh in a while, but when I did, I could tell she was taking mental notes of all of this, and with her training in the FBI, she was already contemplating a plan. She pulled me back down the hallway. We didn't speak until our secret door was closed and we had made our way back to my room. I was mentally and physically exhausted. What were we going to do? Well, I couldn't do anything, but the FBI, CIA, and police would bust in at any moment and shut this place down! Feeling like this would all be over and Sara would be rescued, I lay down on my bed. Exhaustion must have taken over because I did not awaken until the next morning. My dreams were filled with Sara and how much I loved her and how much our friendship meant to me. When I woke up, tears were pouring from my eyes, I just wanted to see my friend and make sure she was ok.

CHAPTER 7

rying and lots of it could be heard from the hallway. Aubrey came in and immediately asked what was going on. I did not have time to tell her about the events of the night before my day shift nurse came in. Swollen eyes, mascara in dark lines down her face, and continued tears as she walked in the door. A feeling of fear and dread swept over me. She started to tell us how Sara, her "favorite physical therapist," had a ruptured appendix and had expired during surgery due to an unforeseen complication. Aubrey started to cry because they had also become close and gotten to know each other. I just sat there in shock. What the hell had happened? Where was Kayleigh? What happened to the FBI? Then the tremors started again. Since all this started, my body had revolted against me and responded to stress in a new way. Uncontrollable tremors, elevated BP, and rapid heart rate was how it started. Panic attacks, and I had no control over them, and that is what really pissed me off. Obviously, when my nurse saw this, she felt horrible, and her first thought was to sedate me. But I was determined to end this and end it now.

Hysterical is probably the best word to describe me for the rest of that day. No one could calm me down, but I did have enough mindset not to blow our cover or say too much. I finally got Aubrey to go to the car and call Agent Johnson and get him to the hospital. When he finally sauntered in, I was livid. I flew questions at him like a gun. He stood there staring at me, and when I calmed down, he spoke. Calm, cool, and carefully, he explained that Sara had not been removed from the hospital. They were watching every aspect closely, hoping to get to the bottom of this horror story. He tried to reason with me and explain that all the time we had put into this would go to waste if we did not find out what the end game was to all of this.

All I could think of was my friend and how she probably felt, how I had felt. But then the agent made a valid point. The only reason I felt anything and woke up at all was that a malfunction in the central line had allowed the medication to leak out. Sara's should be working well, so she would be asleep. In some weird way, this did give me some comfort. At least she wasn't in pain or aware of what was happening; at least she wasn't feeling the same terror I had felt.

When Kayleigh came in for her shift, relief swept over me. Aubrey wanted to stay, but I finally got her to go home. After the commotion of shift change was over, we could talk, and she could update me. She had heard a lot of things that night I had not. Her training became very apparent to me; she was amazing. Memory skills like she possessed had come with extensive training. She was trained to remember specific details and how to filter what was important. The men had talked about multiple women, and they were all supposed to meet in two nights. The reason they had to take Sara was to make up for losing me. We had no idea what this meant.

The plan was for Kayleigh to go to where the morgue was and hide. She would wait until they came to get her body and follow to see what was happening. She wore a wire, and of course, the other agents had been briefed and were on standby for immediate action. Still, I felt uneasy and scared. Even when she reassured me, I had a nagging feeling that this would not end well. Once again, my sixth sense was firing at 180 percent. I just knew something horrible was about to happen.

Man, I hated it when I was right!

CHAPTER 8

Kayleigh was a travel nurse; she did have other patients and assignments. We had been lucky up until this point with her assignments. She had always been on the rehab floor and had me as one of her patients. None of the other nurses wanted to take care of me; they felt awkward, so they gladly handed me over. But this night was different: there had been a huge influenza outbreak, and the hospital was packed. The nursing supervisor had pulled her to the ER to help. This was horrible—who would keep an eye on Sara? This was the first sign of panic I had seen on her face. She did not know what to do, and as our luck would have it, the supervisor that night was a witch. She gave her no time for phone calls or anything. She could not blow her cover, so I watched her walk away. *Okay, stay calm*, I repeated to myself over and over. I had to do something. Anxiously, I waited until the other night shift nurse had her big butt up at the desk, dozing like she always did, and I quietly went down the hall. The morgue was on the other side of the hospital, so I tried to look as normal as I could, but of course, eyes were all over me. My façade of weakness and need for physical therapy would be gone after tonight. But my only priority was Sara and making sure she was okay.

I am no FBI agent, but I have watched enough movies to know that I could not just bust into the room and have a look. I decided to use the benefit of the old back halls once again to my advantage. I went out an emergency exit door and went into a restricted area. This once again led me to a back hallway and practically secret way into the morgue. No one would see me come or go, and I felt sure that I could watch without being noticed. I wondered how Kayleigh planned on doing this, and I was proud of myself for concocting such a smart plan.

Good Lord, I hate spiders. You would have thought a hospital would not have so many, but I guess a closed-off old area did. I had to bite my tongue to not scream a few dozen times. After what seemed like hours, I finally found the way to a small panel. If memory served me correctly, it should go directly to the morgue. When I pulled the panel back, the area was small; I would have to crawl for about fifty feet to get to the part of the morgue. But what if my memory was wrong? It was dark in there, closed in, and I hadn't been in total darkness since "the night." What if I had a panic attack in there? The only light I had was my cell phone, and I hadn't charged it, and I knew it would not last long. My heart started to race—what should I do?

I have always hated how the woman screams, runs, and trips in horror movies. The monster gets her and kills her. She could have a gun or knife, and the killer would get it out of her weak little frail female hand. I always thought I would run faster or just turn and kick the monster's butt. But let me assure you when you are faced with monsters, it is very different. I guess I owe what happened next to Agent Johnson, who told me once that I was a strong woman and to act like it because I did get control of myself and went into that tight, dark crawl space. Looking back, I still can't believe I did it. The space was longer than I had thought, but I started to hear voices and knew I was in the right area. Deciding to go was the best decision of my life because they were there, getting ready to move Sara. My view was limited; I was literally laid flat in a large air vent across from a stretcher. Sara had the IV line in her groin. She was naked, bruised, and she looked dead. I could feel the panic start to stir within me, but I quickly composed myself. My friend needed me; I had to save her no matter what. These were the same four men from the OR. Pierce and the man who had been doing the procedures; I assumed he was a surgeon. Also, a tall, older man who had done the anesthesia, along with a younger man who had been the scrub nurse. I did not recognize any of them at all, except for Pierce.

They were talking about Sara like she was a piece of meat. They would lift her arm, examine her breasts, the taller man would talk about her biopsy results—all normal, of course—and how great her heart looked. They would, in a sexual way, look at her body. She was young and beautiful. She exercised daily and was in amazing physical condition. I could not help but think they got a much better deal with her than me because I was forty, not in great shape, and my breasts were far from perky. I watched them examine her, look in her mouth at her teeth, examine her breasts, then go down to her vagina and inspect it. I was shaking and didn't even realize it. She was violated and probed by these psychotic men, but why? I could only pray that her IV was infusing correctly and she could not feel or hear anything. They violated every orifice my beautiful friend had. Tears filled my eyes, and anger boiled up within my core. If I had a gun in that ugly blue jogging suit, I swore those psychopaths would have been dead.

Time seemed to go slowly, but when they received a phone call, the momentum seemed to change. My back was killing me, my right leg had fallen asleep long ago, but shifting was out of the question. I was afraid they might hear me. When the phone call came, they quickly covered Sara up and moved her to a different stretcher. She would not be going to the funeral home; she had donated her body to science, so her husband had already said his goodbye, and the memorial service would be without her body. She always joked that she refused to have people come around and stare at her dead body and say, "Oh, she looks so good!" I was impressed that he had respected her wishes. The cart to move her was large and bulky, not like a normal stretcher. I assumed they used this to hide the IV pump and meds they were using to keep her sedated. My mind raced—what was I going to do? I looked at my phone. Of course, no signal in there, and I had 16 percent left. I needed to get in touch with Kayleigh or someone immediately. But time was running out; she was being moved. I had about a three-minute break where there was no one in the room, so I reacted without really thinking. I kicked the vent cover off, drug myself across the floor, and climbed under the bottom of the cart. Luckily, I fit, and if they didn't pick up the large plastic cover that was standard in covering up a corpse, I would not be seen.

My plan worked like a charm; I lay under the cart undetected when they came back in. They rolled Sara and me out to a hearse and loaded us in. The IV pump was right beside my head; I could see what they were infusing. One bag was Pancuronium—I was correct, a neuromuscular blocker or paralytic agent—but there was another bag, Versed. This is also a drug used with anesthesia, and it causes amnesia. Relief washed over me; at least Sara would not remember anything that was happening to her. The ride seemed to take forever, so I knew I had a very small window to tell someone what had happened. I texted Kayleigh and explained what had transpired and what I was doing.

Anger probably is not the word I would think to use in describing what her reaction would be. I told her to try to locate my phone signal, but knowing my battery was dying, I hoped she saw the message sooner rather than later, or that would not work.

The ride seemed smooth, like we were on an interstate. The only noise was the hum of the infusion pump. My mind wondered, *What in the world is going on? How is this happening right under the nose of the authorities and the hospital?* My phone had died a little while ago. I'd lost track of time, but I did get to send one more text to my family.

Tripp and Aubrey, I am sorry. I know you have both been through hell the last few weeks. I hope you understand why I had to try to help Sara. I could not bear to think about this happening to another person. There is no way of knowing if I will survive whatever is facing Sara and me, but I wanted to tell you both how much I love you.

Tripp, you are an amazing husband. I love you so much; you have been a great husband, father, and my best friend. I was so worried that when Aubrey left for college, we would grow apart. But we have only gotten closer, and for that, I am so grateful. You are truly my soul mate and the love of my life.

Aubrey, baby, I am sorry for all of this. You are the best daughter a mother could ever ask for. I am so proud of you. The young woman you have become will make some man a wonderful wife and mother. Please stay strong; don't let fear overcome what you know is right. That's what I am doing now. I hope and pray to see you both soon, but if I don't, please remember that we will meet again in Heaven! Love, Mama

CHAPTER 9

ack at the hospital, the ER had been a madhouse. Admissions lined the hallway, and Kayleigh had barely even gotten a bathroom break. She tried to keep her mind on the tasks at hand: shots, labs, and IV starts. But her mind was on her other task, the investigation at the hospital. When she finally got a small break, she looked at her phone and saw the message I had left her. It was too late; the battery had died, and they could not locate my phone. She immediately called Agent Johnson, who had been notified of the hearse leaving but had assumed it was another death due to the fact he hadn't heard from her. Kayleigh was furious. Were these men incompetent? Why had they not followed the vehicle? But I guess he was right—it was a hospital, and patients do die.

Fear gripped everyone; the agent made sure Kayleigh was dismissed from the ER as soon as she was able. Then they all met in the building next door to get an idea of what to do next. They had no idea where they were heading with Sara and me, or how to proceed next. They had discovered that in other hospitals all over the nation where Dr. Pierce had worked, there had been multiple deaths. Odd cases of young women dying but no signs of foul play. There had been no reason to investigate. There was something not right about him, but no one knew what it was. He was only a small piece of a large and complicated puzzle. No one knew yet how large.

Finally, something went right for me. When we arrived at the destination, we were rolled into a holding room. I had a moment to slip out and hide under a small couch. Right as I finished getting my leg under, they came in and checked Sara's medication. Once my eyes adjusted, I could see we were in what looked like a small waiting area. There were two small couches, and it was small but very elaborately decorated, so I knew this was not a hospital setting. I could hear multiple voices now—not just a few, more of a crowd gathering in an adjoining room.

The door opened, and two older women came in with small bags. They did not speak and kept their heads down. Sara's body was uncovered, once again exposing her frailness and vulnerability. One woman brushed her hair, taking time to pull it around her face and shape it nicely. She did have great hair. Then she washed her face and applied a light coat of makeup. She even applied pale pink lip gloss. Neither one spoke; they moved methodically and with purpose, obviously having done this many times before. The other woman washed Sara's body. She applied lotion to her skin and concealer where there were bruises. She was shaved, and her nails were cut and painted. To my disgust, great attention was given to the grooming of her genitals. She was waxed and cleaned with some type of antiseptic soap. A Foley catheter was inserted to remove the urine from her bladder and an enema to clean out her bowels. This process lasted for at least a couple of hours. When they had completed their gruesome task, I was finally able to reposition myself. When I did this, I saw something that made my heart fill with joy: a phone charger. Someone had left a charger plugged into the wall; I slowly and quietly moved over to grab it and was able to get the end to the couch. I plugged my phone in and prayed that they would still be trying to track my location.

Plugging in my phone was a great idea—they could track me—but it was also the reason I was found. I had not even realized I had been discovered when I was pulled by my leg out from under the couch and quickly restrained. I was terrified, and when Dr. Pierce came in, I knew I had made the biggest mistake of my life. He laughed so hard he couldn't speak. Finally, after maintaining his composure, he congratulated me for doing the impossible. He had done this for a long time, he bragged, and I almost ruined it for him. But since I was so ignorant, he was going to make double the money now. He was elated with my presence, not concerned at all about being discovered. He went into detail explaining that being an internal medicine doctor was a profession that did not provide him with the finances to live the lavish lifestyle he desired. He would surface somewhere in the US or Europe once a year and make enough money to "relax" the rest of the time.

As he spoke and boasted of his psychotic career, I was re-strained, and the men I had seen before came in. Thrilled to see me and quick to work, an IV was placed in my arm. I fought as much as I could, but I was no match for these men. I was not paralyzed, just sedated mildly. I could hear and feel but could not put up a fight. He directed them to "prepare me," and as I lay on a bed beside Sara, the women reappeared and started to work on me.

I was shaved, washed, and, like Sara, makeup applied. They evacuated my bowels and emptied my bladder as they had Sara. I would fall into a twilight sleep to awaken when they would move me or do something painful. Trying to keep my eyes open was close to impossible. I wanted to see these wom-en, to get them to help us. But they functioned like robots, with no emotional response to their nefarious task at hand. The men came back after I was sufficiently prepared and did the inspection I had witnessed on Sara earlier. All I could do was pray that the agent or Kayleigh would bust in and rescue me, but this did not happen. They went over my labs, my bi-opsy, and the testing I'd had. It wasn't as recent as they liked to have on hand, but "good enough," they felt. My legs were spread open as they inspected my genitals while another was commenting on my breasts. I was violated in a way no one could ever describe. Praying for death was all I could do. I tried to think of something else, focus on something else; nothing could take me from the terror I was in. Being violated in this manner, helpless and sedated, I prayed as hard as I could for unconsciousness.

Finally, when the process was finished, Sara and I were laid side by side, naked. She was chemically restrained, but I had on wrist restraints. The tall anesthesiologist had started an IV drip that was making me come in and out of consciousness.

After what felt like hours of going in and out of sleep, I was rolled down a long hallway. The lights were so bright; it was so cold. I had essentially given up at this point. I wanted death to come and come swiftly. I have two sets of grandparents waiting for me in Heaven, and I was not afraid to die. I just did not want to fight any longer. I wanted this nightmare to be over. Of course, I was sad for my family left behind. Would Tripp remarry? I hoped so; he deserves to be happy. I prayed for my beautiful daughter to find a great man and have a wonderful life. I didn't want to miss her wedding or never meet my grandchildren, but I could not escape what was happening.

They stopped in a large open room. I tried to look around and see what was surrounding me. When I got my eyes to focus, I could not believe what I was seeing. This had to be some type of dream.

Human trafficking is a $32 billion annual industry. It is estimated that 800,000 women and children are trafficked a year across international borders. The women are used as sexual slaves or forced into prostitution. Then you have the opposite issue of organ trafficking. The demand for organs is very high. It is estimated that there are over 123,000 men, women, and children awaiting organs right now. Some hospitals and funeral homes have been caught with illegal organ trafficking at alarming numbers. An average healthy person could save up to eight lives if they could donate everything. Apparently, these greedy psychopaths had taken these two industries and made it into an open market, so to speak. As I looked around me, I saw around twenty beds with naked women on them. Some younger and some older, but none over forty. All small in stature, very healthy appearing, and some light skinned and some dark. The room was elaborate, with large vases of flowers everywhere. Crystal chandeliers hung, and soft music played. I was reminded of an art auction. Young men in tuxedos carried hors d'oeuvres on trays, and Moet & Chandon Dom Perignon Champagne. Leather chairs were lining the walls where men and women of all ages sat. They drank and ate and laughed like they were at a party.

Eventually, the man I recognized as the surgeon addressed the audience. He welcomed everyone and explained that he thought this was one of the "best auctions of the year!" The crowd applauded, and I felt my heart pounding in my head. He spoke about the value of "live specimens" and bragged that no "specimen" could be tracked. All transactions were anonymous and discrete; all services were carried out by board-certified surgeons.

He started at the beginning of the line and presented each woman. He stated their age and went through the results of the testing they had undergone. I could not help but think of an auto auction. He went into detail about their childbearing capability or if they had already given birth. The distinguished members of the audience took notes as he spoke. I was last; I listened as he went over Sara and they came to me.

He explained that I was not as sedated as the other ladies but would cooperate just fine. He briefly discussed that organ procurement from a live donor was much better than from a cadaver, and since surgeons and physicians were handling this, the results would be outstanding. He reassured them that no one would be investigating, that the "subjects had already been declared dead." I wondered, did he forget me? I was in shock; he was selling our organs or our bodies at an auction. Why did someone not figure this out? How did the FBI miss this? The buyers could either be here procuring an organ for a loved one or themselves or purchase one of us for sexual slavery. I could see many men who were from foreign countries, but what astounded me the most was the number of women present at this "body auction."

Next was a time for the buyers to have a closer look. They all walked around the beds, looked at us, touched us, and discussed us like we were cattle at a farm. Waiters in tuxedos walked around offering more juicy morsels of delicate finger foods. A wealthy-appearing older lady and man came over to my stretcher. They were discussing needing a heart-lung transplant for their son, who had severe pulmonary hypertension. I was the correct blood type, but so was Sara. But before they arrived, an Arabic man had shown interest in Sara for sexual pleasure. He had touched her all over and inspected her in such a perverse way I closed my eyes. This process continued for quite some time, but eventually, they were directed to return to their seats. Since I was not paralyzed and could move, I had tried to wiggle loose from my restraints, but the medication had me so drowsy I could not. Being in and out of consciousness allowed me to hear the auction start. Some of us had multiple bids. People spoke up and would ask for certain things; one lady wanted a kidney from the third woman, but a man wanted her lungs. The "specimens," as we were referred to, chosen for sexual trafficking took the longest. The buyers wanting organ procurement would fight over their organs, so the price continued to climb. Even in my drugged stupor, I was amazed at the money being offered. These sick, deranged men had taken two very illegal enterprises and were making millions by putting them into one huge body auction.

Time seemed to drag on and on until the auctioneer of death stood over me. I started to panic. I felt my heart speed up; beads of sweat started popping out on my forehead. They must have noticed because all it took was a wave of his hand for me to get a nice dose of IV Valium. The last thing I remembered was the bid for my heart and lungs and a comment that my liver biopsy had revealed mild hepatic steatosis, or fatty liver. That really pissed me off; I knew I should have laid off the ice cream and cookies! Those darned drug reps always bought those lunches. I mean, I can't help my liver is a little "fatty"!

When I awoke, I came to the realization that my life was ending. I was going to be taken to an OR and literally have my organs removed while I was alive. In the large room, some women had already been removed, but it seemed like those of us for organ procurement were still there. We had been alone in the room for a few hours when I heard a door open; I didn't even care to try to look any longer. I knew my end was near and was resigned to it, glad I'd sent that last text to my family. Then the pain and pull of the IV being ripped out of my arm made me look, and to my surprise, Kayleigh was kneeling beside me. She had given me something in my IV before pulling it out. Immediately, I felt a jolt of energy; she had given me Romazicon, the reversal of Valium.

Sitting up rapidly was a bad idea; my head went in circles, and nausea overcame me. She helped me get off the stretcher, and we quickly started unhooking the other women. Kayleigh was calm and focused on the task, all the time explaining that the men had left with only minimal security and they had "taken care" of them. The FBI hoped to have the building set up as a trap and arrest the physicians and the people helping them carry this out. Also, the "buyers" were to be back the next night to settle with payments and details, and they would be trapped. For the first time in weeks, I had a glimmer of hope.

It wasn't long before more FBI agents arrived and helped the lethargic women out; they could not walk and needed to be carried. At that point, I realized I was also still nude. This was made even worse when Agent Johnson walked in. He came up beside me and ask how I was, concern on his masculine face. Taking his jacket off and placing it over my shoulders made me even more embarrassed. My skin flushed despite the coolness of the room when the tall, muscular agent touched my bare shoulder. An electrical current went down my body, and quickly my brain knew how inappropriate this was.

Soon, we were all loaded into FBI vans and taken to a hospital nearby. I was crying and didn't even realize it until Kayleigh grabbed my hand. My first question was what had happened to the other women who had been taken out; she hung her head and reported that they had already been removed before they arrived. Sara was okay; she was just starting to wake up. She started to cry, shake, and panic. I knew exactly how she felt; my heart broke for her. Somewhat like a clumsy toddler trying to walk, I got up off my stretcher and rolled close to her. Lying practically on top of her, I held her, rubbed her hair, comforted her, neither of us caring that we were cold and nude, just needing comfort. All you could hear was sobbing in the van, the weeping because we were rescued and glad to be alive, but also for those women who had not been rescued in time. Despite the anesthetics, the women had heard some pieces of conversations and were aware of what was happening to them.

Once at the hospital, we were all separated; IV fluids were quickly administered to help flush the drugs out of our bodies. We were all malnourished and very weak. The others would need rehab and physical therapy just like I had needed. I, however, was fine after getting fluids and some food. Seeing Tripp and Aubrey run through the doors made everything 100 percent better.

Hours passed, and there were no updates on what was happening. Sara's husband knocked on my door, and he couldn't even speak; he just cried and hugged me for the longest time. No words were needed. He finally did get out, "Thank you!"

We heard nothing overnight; the hospital was a constant flood of FBI agents and police. Tripp informed me that they had closed the ER off to all other emergency traffic and diverted to another ER close by. The government's handpicked physicians replaced the ER physicians. No one could be trusted, and this was a very delicate matter, per Agent Johnson. The screams of relief came in waves from people who were reunited with their sisters, spouses, and other family members. Imagine getting a call in the middle of the night that your loved one who was thought to be dead was actually alive. These families had witnessed their loved ones be buried and had mourned them. I cannot imagine how they felt at that moment when what they had thought was lost was returned to them.

These women had been from all over; some families would not arrive for twelve or more hours. Emotions ran wild that night. Screams of panic, relief, terror, sadness could be heard for hours. These physicians and nurses may have been sent from a military facility, but in all my years, I have never experienced more compassion and caring. When we were examined for sexual assault per protocol and questioned, they tried to be as gentle and respectful as they could. Kayleigh was always close to Sara or me, going in between our rooms, checking on us. Sometime during the next morning, I finally fell asleep for what seemed like days.

The next forty-eight hours were a barrage of questions, especially for me. Since I was the only person who had been somewhat lucid and able to see and hear what exactly was taking place, they needed all the details I could provide. The various agencies spent the day planning the stakeout. They had "taken care of" the guards, which left the building empty until the masterminds returned to prepare for the transactions to take place. I was on edge all day, waiting and wondering what would happen. Would they catch them? Would they escape? I just could not comprehend that this practice of evil body trading would continue another day.

I tried to see Sara a couple of times, but she was either sleeping or with the therapists. They had assigned therapists to come by and talk to each of us and see how we were holding up.

Aubrey once again was a rock; she never left my side. Tripp was in and out, trying to help with food and support. I started to notice Kayleigh hadn't been in for a few hours. When I enquired, I was told she had left and it was confidential. Irritated by this, I kept walking around the ER. Her leaving was odd to me. Then it hit me: she was at the stakeout.

When the detectives came by later in the afternoon, I had the opportunity to ask questions. I wanted to know how they would get Pierce and the others in the room and set it up. I quickly wished I hadn't asked!

CHAPTER 10

Nausea, panic, and other emotions flooded me when I was told the events that were to take place. The FBI where having female agents act as decoys. They had attempted to find women who would closely enough match the women for sale. But this was impossible; they would probably "prepare" them again before they were due to be released to the buyers. Then they would know, and it would be over before the sale went down. As much as I wanted Pierce, I wanted those sick buyers to be punished also. They had three hours before time, and every second mattered. A road construction crew was set up to make sure no one arrived unannounced. I could see the uncertainty in the eyes of the detectives; this plan had not been well thought out and had an enormous potential of going wrong. One thing the agencies all want is control, and they did not have it.

I was going crazy sitting, waiting, and not knowing what would happen. The fact that Kayleigh was a decoy disturbed me. She was my friend; I loved her and was afraid for her. She had given me hope when I had none, encouragement when I needed it, and had no problem pushing me to heal my mind as well as my body. I owed her a debt I could never repay. But what could I do? My mind raced; I had to help somehow.

I was fine; I wasn't weak from the drugs, like the other women. I felt normal. After much thought, when my panic subsided, I had an idea, but the problem would be how to get everyone to go along with it.

The first person I explained my plan to had been a female detective whom I had only met since I had been here. Her name was Asia. She worked as a secretary in the ER but was like a lot of these hospital employees, an undercover agent. Asia was young, perky, and hilarious. She made us all laugh so much, and it helped to get our minds off the horrible situation we were in. Just guessing her age, I would not say over twenty-five—not old enough to be an agent. Curiosity had gotten the best of me, and I had enquired about her from another nurse. She explained to me that she was a computer genius, had graduated college at sixteen, and had been quickly recruited into the FBI. She was an amazing woman, and the best part was you would have never guessed what hid behind that innocent personality.

When I had a moment alone, I went out to the desk and asked her to talk to me. To the average person needing medical care, the ER looked normal. But it had, indeed, been taken over and closed to routine ER visits. The ER had been placed on "divert," which meant the EMS knew not to come here, and the sore throats, abdominal pains, headaches, etc., were all sent away to the nearest Urgent Care. I could not help but wonder how this hospital's administration felt about this situation. The healthcare system had become so money-driven because of the new laws. They were sure to lose revenue with this shutdown. The thought of administrators at their mahogany desks, in expensive suits, sweating over this, did make me smile a little.

When she came in, she had that amazing smile on her face, but it quickly turned into a serious scowl when I began to explain my plan. Getting her to listen was the hard part; she was quite a talker. I knew they had placed me nearest the door at the auction; I would be the first one to be seen. If the fake road construction crew could stall long enough and make it possible that the buyers and the sellers arrived at the same time, they would not have time to reinspect the product, so to speak. I pleaded my case with her and explained I was fine; I had made it this far. I was not weak, and I had to have closure or I would never recover from this. This was something I would have to see for myself, not just hear from someone else. I had to be there and see this end.

The feeling that something was not right, someone else was involved, kept nagging at me.

She listened, interrupted often, but I quickly came back with a reason why my plan was the best option for succeeding. She knew it was true but hated to admit it. Government agencies do not like to use civilian persons to help, especially when they have no experience and have already been kidnapped twice. But let's face it, I was a pro now.

After much argument and tears, she agreed to call the detective on the case and run it by him. Aubrey came in at the end, and Asia stopped the conversation and left. In my mind, I debated on whether to tell her my proposal, but I was afraid of what she would say. I had put my poor husband and daughter through hell. I knew it wasn't my fault, but how could I ask her to worry more? She knew by my face I was up to something, so I spilled it. If looks could kill, I would have died after the first two sentences. But after I explained in detail, she understood. Her only request was that she could be close to me. She wanted to be in the FBI van down the road. I did not like that idea at all, but this was her condition, and this would not be changed.

After a few minutes, Asia came back with an update. She informed me that they had very reluctantly agreed. The best chance of making this work was to use me. The events that followed this seemed to happen in warp speed.

CHAPTER 11

How in God's name did I end up back on this stretcher, naked and cold? I must have lost my mind. But I found comfort knowing that Kayleigh and multiple other women were lying beside me in the room, and they were armed. This place was surrounded, and the roadblock had worked great. The buyers and sellers would arrive together. The caveat to all of this was that to arrest the buyers, the deals had to be in process, or they could lie and make up another reason for being there. They had to be caught in the act, so to speak. This was where I was afraid things would fall apart. For what seemed like hours, we lay there, quiet and trying not to move. I admit I was excited; I hate that because this was a sick and horrible situation. I guess it was the adrenaline and the rush to get the bad guys.

When I heard the door open, I tried to barely breathe; it was Pierce. Just as I had predicted, since my stretcher was first in line, he checked and reported that all was going well and as planned. My plan worked; they didn't have time to make any changes or do anything to us again. The sale was about to take place. We were rolled out into the large room where the original auction had taken place. The lights were dim; once again, low music played. There must have been huge vases of roses in the room because the aroma was potent. The smell of the roses was repugnant; I wanted to vomit.

The medical staff had made the IVs and fake medications look very real. No one knew these were not the original women. But that didn't last long.

Pierce welcomed everyone once again. He explained payment methods, how satisfied he knew they were going to be with the purchases, and when the next auction would be. (I thought, *Yeah, right, you sick bastard!*) But my heart fell when I heard one man ask to "view his purchase one more time." This was it. I wanted to look, open my eyes, and turn my head, but I could not. Obviously, he was permitted to, and he took his time being polite, speaking to the other buyers when he made his way. The next thing I heard was, "What the hell?" After this, things happened at the speed of light. Immediately, I heard him yell; then Pierce yelled out a stream of profanity. At this point, I opened my eyes and looked around at the chaos. Agents came from nowhere and stormed the room. People tried to run, but the doors were already blocked. The agents jumped off the beds and had guns drawn before I could even sit up. I was truly amazed at the speed and efficiency of the half-nude female agents. Everything was smooth, and in a flash, these sick, depraved people were up against the wall in the room and being cuffed. The lights were turned on, and I could finally visualize the surroundings. The last time I'd been too lethargic to be very observant, but now I could evaluate the room. I had been correct; multiple huge vases had those malodorous roses in them. They looked expensive. Crystal chandeliers hung from the ceiling. There were high-top tables with champagne and crystal glasses; I assumed they were awaiting a toast to the recent purchases the buyers had made.

I snapped out of it when I heard my name; Kayleigh was yelling at me. I guess I was in shock at the chaos taking place around me. I turned to look at her, and I saw the look of panic on her face. At that moment, the man who had been the anesthesiologist came out of nowhere. He must not have been where the FBI had projected because when he grabbed me, everyone was shocked. He had his arm around my neck and a gun to my temple before anyone knew what had happened.

It was possibly due to the events of the last few weeks, but I swear, I wasn't panicking. Poor Kayleigh looked terrified, and Agent Johnson also looked surprised at this unexpected turn of events. I could feel the cold, hard end of the gun pressed against my temple. His respiratory rate was rapid, and his breath had a sweet, sickening smell to it. His pulse was racing, and I think he was more nervous than me.

He demanded that the others be released or he would kill me. After all, I had been nothing but trouble this whole time. He explained that he wasn't bluffing—he didn't care to shoot me at all; it would be his pleasure. I guess everyone knew he was serious because they slowly started putting their weapons down and letting the buyers and sellers go. The buyers ran as fast as they could from the room. However, the doctors stood there, and in an instant, they had the weapons and the agents as well as me up against the walls. I was amazed at how the circumstances had changed so quickly. As I looked around, the female agents were in their thongs and topless, due to the staging needed. Yet still, I was eerily calm—I mean, of course, nervous—but not terrified at all. The thought of death had become a familiar acquaintance to me, and here I was, looking my old friend in the face once again.

They were not sure what to do; they had no doubt that there were more FBI agents outside, but remember, these were physicians, not police or FBI. They were nervous and knew that they did not have the upper hand. Kayleigh knew this because it was her that made the first move. She looked around and gave another female agent a look and head-butted the man behind her as hard as she could. Immediately after a large crack, blood poured from his nose. He screamed a loud, girlish scream and let her go to grab his broken nose. Just like a well-played-out plan, when the other men looked in shock, the other agents took that moment to attack. Once again, my brain couldn't keep up with the events that happened so quickly. I so wished I could see things in slow motion like in a movie; that way, I could see who did what.

At some point, Agent Johnson was fighting with Pierce for a gun. They went back and forth until a horrible sound erupted. The gun went off, but where did the bullet go? Then I saw a beautiful lady fall to the floor. She was one of the agents who had been playing a part in this sick play. She was blond and had long locks of hair cascading down her back. Her naked breasts were perky and young. Skin white as the white roses in the vase near her. She was wearing a pale blue thong, and a small tattoo was on her lower back. A small crimson line of blood ran from her right upper chest as she crumbled to the floor. I screamed out; I wanted everyone to stop and help her, but the chaos continued.

I assumed the FBI vans outside had heard the shot because in seconds, more agents arrived, shots fired, screams rang out, and then I had a feeling I had never had. In my mid-back, between my shoulders, a hot fiery feeling. It felt like a branding iron had been stuck between my shoulders. I stood there, looking ridiculous, I suppose, and everyone looked at me with mouths gaping open. What the heck were they staring at? I was tired and ready to go home; this day had been exhausting, and I was dizzy at this point. Kayleigh ran to me and helped me lie down. I tried to tell her I didn't need to lie down when she explained I had been shot. That ridiculous man had shot me in the back.

CHAPTER 12

Six months flew by. I could not remember anything after I passed out on the floor. Multiple sellers were either injured or dead. Three agents died, and I came very close once again. After a long, extensive surgery, the bullet was removed, and miraculously, it had missed every major organ. Recovery was long and hard, but I got stronger every day. The other ladies were never found. One good thing was a log had been kept of the buyers, their bids, and other details. They were all arrested and charged. That demon Pierce was shot but did not die. However, I was certain he would have chosen death. He was shot in the spine, which resulted in him becoming quadriplegic. He became a total care patient. He cannot so much as lift his own finger to care for himself. Kept alive by a ventilator, fed by tubes, bathed and taken care of by strangers. He was placed in a state institution, and I called that *karma*! I hated to admit it, but I hoped he suffered every single day.

I was hesitant to return to work. The time just had not come that I felt I could handle it. Kayleigh kept in touch often, and Sara was back at work and was expecting a baby! She recovered quickly and was back to her normal, perky self. The new baby had given her a new focus and something to be excited and happy about. Just a side note: that baby was conceived in the stairwell between the second and third floor!

Tripp took a new job and traveled a lot. I worried that this trauma had affected him more than he wanted to admit. He seemed more distant. Before the events happened, Aubrey was undecided about her career, but she decided on FBI training. She had already completed her four-year bachelor's degree from Appalachian State University, and with her new friends and a few strings pulled, she got into the academy. It scared me, but I had never seen her happier or more energetic.

I knew I needed to go back, but I got that sick panic feeling at the thought of walking into the hospital. Smelling that antiseptic odor, hearing the noises in a hospital setting—all of it scared me to death. I still could not shake that something was not right. That a person had gotten away who shouldn't have, that someone was still out there. The therapist explained to me that it was PTSD (post-traumatic stress disorder), but I was not convinced that was my diagnosis. In the back of my mind always were those women who were not saved. Where were they? Were they dead; were they alive and being used as a sexual commodity? Sometimes when Kayleigh, Sara, and I went to dinner, we thought of them, said a prayer for them, and wept for them.

Tripp was home the weekend I finally decided to go back to work. I had tried to be "normal" more often and not act like a crazy person. Don't get me wrong, he was always understanding, but I had not been able to be intimate since this all started. He had always been a very sexual man. He felt the way to show love and affection was through sex and intimacy. It is well known and a documented fact that a man's thought process is the opposite of a woman's. I need him to help me around the house, tell me I'm pretty, and things like that to feel loved. He just wants me to focus all my feelings on sex. I had a lot of panic and fear issues and just could not be intimate. But I decided we had to get back to normal. Prior to this, we had a great sex life for a married couple in their forties. Aubrey being at college had rekindled a spark, and we could experiment more.

So, before he got home, I took a long bubble bath. Cleaned up the "downtown" area, if you know what I mean, and placed candles all over the house. I put a note on the door that had him follow a candlelit path to the bedroom, where I had on a very small piece of lingerie. Our favorite songs played on my "lovemaking" playlist. The mood was set, and he was excited. His face was lit up, smiling wide as a Cheshire cat. My heart melted with love for him, that sweet face and smile. At that moment, I didn't remember why I had held out so long. I wanted him; I needed him. His arms needed to be around me, holding me tight and keeping me safe.

That night was like no other in our twenty years of marriage. He needed me as much as I needed him. He ravaged me; he made love to me; and he made me feel sexy, loved, and safe all in one night.

After hours, we realized we were starving and needed some food. We went to the kitchen at about 2:00 a.m. and made some omelets. We laughed and talked and had the best time we'd had in years. It was like the horror had never happened. The events were forgotten for this night. I was happier than I can express in words.

Eventually, when we had been fully satisfied in every way and were exhausted, we went to bed. For a while, I just laid my head on his chest, and we held each other. He kissed me deeply on my mouth, down my neck, on my breasts, and down my stomach. The only thing that was mentioned about the events of the previous year was when he kissed my abdomen and the small scar where my liver biopsy had been. He looked up at me, smiled, and said, "I think you have a great liver, baby, and I know it's not fatty." We both laughed and fell asleep holding each other. Safe and happy were feelings I had not had the luxury to have in many months, and right before a blanket of deep sleep covered me, I thanked God for letting us survive.

The next morning in the shower, I sang and was so happy. My mind replayed the previous evening; it had been so wonderful. As I bathed my still thin body, I happened to see the small puncture wound on my right upper abdomen. Laughing to myself about Tripp's comment regarding my "fat liver," the strangest thing happened. Before my brain processed what was happening, it was like my body reacted. The first thing was my hands; they started to tremble so hard my hot-pink sponge fell from them. Then, despite being in the hot shower and sweat pouring from my forehead, I had a chill that went to my bones.

Waves of nausea caused me to have dry heaves, and then I realized, in utter terror, Tripp had no way of knowing about that report. That had never been discussed in front of him.

No, *no*, I had to be mistaken. I was in and out of sleep and on anti-anxiety meds at that time; he'd had to hear or read it somewhere. This was my husband of almost twenty-one years, my best friend, and the father of my daughter. What was wrong with me? Was I insane? Yes, that was it. Going back to work too early had put too much stress on my poor brain.

Like a robot, I got dressed and pushed those horrible thoughts into the furthest recess of my brain. I wanted to look nice. The day would be full of stares, gossip, and speculation. I wanted to appear put together, sane, and for my patient's sake, mentally capable of taking care of them. I put on a cute short dress and Antonio Milani wedges and picked up my lab coat. The symbol of what I do, who I am. I had not worn it for so long, it felt strange and odd to me. Was I ready to go back? Could I face the questions, the looks of pity and wonder? Yes, I could, I had to, I had to get my life back. I called Aubrey on my way to work and told her I loved her, set my blue Mini-Cooper on cruise, and turned my radio wide open.

CHAPTER 13

Walking in wasn't as bad as I had thought. I was greeted with warm smiles, lots of hugs. I must have heard, "You look amazing!" over fifty times. It did take me a while to get back into the routine of things. With the new government regulations, electronic medical records changed often. I needed an update and had to spend a lot of my morning in the IT department. Being proud of myself for my smile that never left and controlling my nausea, I walked down the stairs to the basement. Going down the corridor made me have some serious flashbacks to the night Sara was taken. I ducked into the ladies' locker room, took some deep breaths, and controlled myself. Tears streamed down my face, my makeup ran, and the longer it took, the more irritated I became at myself. I had to look good, normal, and not emotional! After about thirty minutes and some makeup touchups, I was on my way. I got my new passwords, learned the latest updates, and headed up to see my patients.

CCU 15 was a fifty-five-year-old female; she had come in during the night with a drug overdose. She was already waking up and trying to pull her tubes out. I saw her, updated the family, and dictated her note. Okay, I was fine, able to focus—what's the old saying? Like riding a bike? I went down my list of patients, and despite being slower than I used to be, I was fine!

I had always gotten along well with the CCU nurses because that was where I had worked as an RN. These were my friends, my peers, and the best nurses in the hospital. Many of them had been there over twenty years; many had attended my funeral. I had not seen them since that day, and some of them started to tear up as I walked in, but I quickly told them I was fine.

My last patient was a sixty-year-old man, admitted with pneumonia. He had been a heavy smoker and had continued to decline and needed life support. The pulmonologist I was working with that week was one who had only been with the practice for about two years. He was sweet, caring, and enthusiastic. Flowers and messages were sent to me almost weekly since I had been home. I had missed him, and when he grabbed me, hugged me, and gave me his customary kiss on the cheek, I felt back to normal.

It was when I walked into CCU 3 to see this patient that I had my first flashback. I did what I normally did: went over to the ventilator (life support machine) to check the settings. This machine gives you certain amounts of oxygen, pressures to open your lungs, and essentially breathes for you when you are too sick to. When pneumonia becomes worse, the setting must be adjusted. When a patient has improved enough, we wean the settings and can take the tube out. Next, I examine the patient by listening to their lungs, heart and looking for edema (swelling) or any other abnormal findings. The last thing is to check the drips the patients are on. When the patient is this critically ill, they may need multiple IV medications for the maintenance of their blood pressure and always meds for sedation. It is not comfortable to be on life support, so almost all patients are sedated. Some drips just make you sleep. However, some are specifically for pain. As I explained earlier, some medications paralyze your body. This is meant to keep you from fighting against the machines. These drugs are not used often due to the side effects. But Dr. Enrique seemed to use them more often than the other pulmonologists. We had expressed our concern in the past, but in some cases, the use was appropriate to give the patient the best chance of survival.

When I reached up and read the label on the bag, that was when it happened. I felt my heart rate speed up, sweat beads popped out of my forehead, and I started to hyperventilate. I froze, stood there with the bag in my hand, and could not move.

The CCU nurse taking care of the patient that day was a good friend of mine, Heather Hall. She was a short, attractive nurse. Her ICU experience made her confident and sometimes opinionated with what she needed for her patient care. She had long, straight hair, always pulled back. Her voice was loud and often seemed as if she were yelling. Many times, she offended people by her tone and was felt to be very sarcastic.

However, she was a great nurse; she knew her job and did it well. She and I had always gotten along well, and she had even worked in our office at one point. The job of an RN in an office setting is very different than a hospital setting. Not easy, just different, and she had hated it, mainly due to drama in the office, which was a total disorganized hellhole, but that's another story.

Keeping up with the news and knowing some details, she knew what was happening when I froze. The drip in the IV was a paralytic. In an instant, I was back in that coffin. I could smell the roses, feel the satin, cool and soft on my skin. I could not move my legs or speak. Heat ran up my spine as the sweat began to drop from my forehead. I did not realize what was going on until I was sitting on the ground on the ICU floor. Dr. Enrique was yelling my name. Heather was fanning me; everyone was staring at me. I felt the flush of embarrassment cover my face. I felt the cold hardness of the floor on my butt. For a moment, I had no idea what had happened.

Realizing I had a flashback was quite upsetting for me. How could I move past this and get on with my life if I never knew when it would happen? If I smelled a rose, would I flashback? Could I go to the funeral home if someone died? My mind was racing with panic, worry, and the feeling that my mind and body were betraying me. I had always been a control freak, and I was certainly not in control now.

Dr. Enrique walked with me back to the lounge, and I got a drink. He was so concerned and sympathetic to me. He wanted to help me but had no idea what to say or do.

After about an hour, I felt better and offered to go see patients on the floor. I prayed the entire time on the elevator that nothing would trigger another attack. Again, I tried to act normal, confident; I could not let everyone see my fear and pity me. I ignored the stares and put on an act of self-control and confidence. The rest of the day went smoothly, without any further episodes. As I finished up with dictations, anxiety started building because I knew I had to go home and face yet another demon, this one my husband of twenty years.

CHAPTER 14

Tripp was a handsome man. He was not tall, only a small amount taller than I was. His hair was deep brown with some gray sprinkled in, and he had a receding hairline. His face was round and cute with an adorable smile that had always melted my heart. He had a laugh that made me so happy, and in the past few months, I had not heard much of it at all.

I arrived home before him, which was not normal. I typically got home a good two hours after him, but his work had taken him out of town. I prepared a salad and watched the news. I hated watching the news. It was so depressing. Either someone had shot another person or there was yet another political scandal brewing. You could never know what the truth or fiction was.

I sat and thought about how to handle this situation. Not saying anything at all would only make me miserable, and I could not hide my emotions well at all. If I accused him, I risked losing him. After much thought and prayer, I made up my mind what to do.

After he had eaten and taken his place in his leather recliner, I just came right out and asked him, explaining that I did not recall telling him that information and wondering where he had heard it. I tried to not sound like this was an accusation but more like I was just curious. His eyes were wide, mouth hung open, and I could see his mind racing. As this happened, I felt my own heart rate jump to a fast rhythm. I could tell he could not answer without a lot of thought. This was concerning to me—what was there to think about? Unless my original fear was true and he had been involved the whole time. He finally said he must have overheard someone talking about it, and stuttering, he said that he remembered one of the agents talking about it. He was nervous as he spoke, his voice trembling like a child being scolded for spilling something on an expensive rug. I knew immediately he was lying. But I smiled, nodded, and never let him know that inside me brewed a storm of emotion. Devastation, rage, and my heart broke. He seemed convinced that I had believed his ridiculous story and changed the subject to ask me how my day had been. I also lied and told him great, like I had never been away. After a few more minutes of torture, I excused myself to go take a bubble bath and read. He knows nothing makes me happier or more relaxed than a hot bubble bath and a good suspense novel. I had to be alone, think, and clear my head.

As I ran my tub, I texted Kayleigh and let her know I needed to talk to her alone as soon as she could. She was in Arizona working undercover at a large hospital. We talked or texted at least three or four times a week, so I knew she was out of the state. That didn't matter. I had to talk to someone; I had to get another opinion. Was I paranoid or just crazy? If he was truly involved, I could not let him know that I was suspicious. As I reclined back into the soothing water, I took deep breaths to try to calm myself. Why would my beloved husband do this? He seemed to love me; I thought we were happy. I mean, I knew this past year had been hell, but that wasn't directly my fault.

It had to be the money—they were offering him a lot of cash for him to "sell" me. He had always wanted to live at the beach, a tropical paradise. I had refused because I liked the mountains and I would not move so far from my family. But surely he would not go to such lengths?

I had tried to keep up with what was still going on with my case. The FBI was still searching for the other buyers who had left immediately after seeing the "merchandise." Kayleigh had made it her personal job to look for the other women on the side, but it was close to impossible to track dead women. The process of elimination looking for women who had expired where Dr. Pierce had been employed had been a virtual nightmare. Naturally, when the details of what had happened went public, hundreds of families had enquired about their loved ones. Many families had bodies exhumed to be sure. It was emotional torture for so many people. Aubrey searched the training facility when she could to also try to find the other men involved who had gotten away. I was not the only one who felt like Dr. Pierce was not the head of this business. We all felt this was a small arm of a much larger operation. Things that Sara, Kayleigh, and I had heard made us feel like this was a huge, worldwide business. But they had nowhere to start. The men who had not gotten away were dead, and Pierce could not give any information in his state of health. I sometimes felt that they knew much more than they were telling me, but I didn't really dig for details either. I had been trying to put this all behind me and get some semblance of normalcy until this issue with Tripp came up.

CHAPTER 15

I t was a few days later before I could finally update Kayleigh on what had happened. I could not tell her with Tripp home, so with the time difference, it was difficult to talk to her. Attempting to explain what had happened without putting my opinion in the mix was hard. She listened and did not inter- ject until I was done telling her the whole story. She agreed that something was not right. Immediately, she placed a call to Detective Johnson. It had been months since I had heard his name; the last time I saw him was when I was still in the hospital. He had stopped by and told me bye one last time before leaving for his next assignment. Guilt aroused inside of me when she spoke of him. Here I was practically accusing my dear husband of being in the most horrible criminal ring I could imagine, and now I had these inappropriate feelings about another man.

When Kayleigh called me back, she sounded different. Woman have a way of bonding with one another, and we can tell what we are thinking and feeling just by the look on our face or the tone of voice. So, I knew she was upset after hearing her first few words. Kayleigh, with urgency in her voice, said she had to see me and was booking a flight to Charlotte at her first possible chance. That's all she would say. A chill ran through me, I knew she would not leave the case she was on unless things were bad. I was advised to act normal and not tell anyone what was going on. Not sure about this, especially when it came to Aubrey, I attempted to carry on with my life as normal. Kayleigh could not give me a definite time when she would arrive.

Going to work got easier as the days passed. The nurses didn't stare and whisper as often, and no panic attacks hit unexpectedly. At home, Tripp and I ate dinner, worked, and life was somewhat stable. We fell back into the normal routine of watching our favorite Netflix series, and things seemed normal. Looming in the back recess of my mind was the possibility of his involvement.

After a few days, when Kayleigh took care of other business, she arrived. I was concerned because it had taken her longer to arrive than we had originally thought. Tripp didn't seem suspicious when I let him know I was meeting her for dinner. We had gotten together so much in the past few months, it wasn't out of the norm.

The restaurant was a small sushi bar that was great. The atmosphere was awesome—dim lights and trendy décor. The best part was the booths located in the back, which were very private. We could talk and not worry about being overheard by anyone. After ordering drinks and appetizers, I was anxious to get into the details of what she had discovered. She did not waste any time letting me know that they could not find any record of Tripp being in contact with Dr. Pierce. They hacked into his personal and work computers, and nothing came up. But one thing that concerned them was that when he traveled so much, he seemed to always find a computer to use. For example, at the hotel, he would go to the lobby and use the "quest computers." Very odd because he always had his own personal laptop to use. Because of the hotel servers, it was almost impossible to know what or who he had contacted. They were trying to look at hotel surveillance videos and the times he logged in. This would take some time to do, and all they could do was wait.

She did know for certain that no one, including Detective Johnson or herself, had divulged details of the case with Tripp. They were careful not to talk about specifics in front of him at the hospital. They felt certain he had not overheard or been informed in any way about my liver biopsy results. Once again, I had that panic feeling, but over the last few weeks, I had been able to get control of that monster that hid within me. I quickly controlled it and listened to Kayleigh. The options were clear. They could take Tripp in and let him know that he was being investigated, which could end my marriage, or the façade could continue until more details were known. The choice was mine, but I could tell that the agency wanted to try to catch other participants, and this may be the way in.

Still, a small glimmer of hope was in my soul. When I finally got the courage to ask her, I immediately regretted it. Did they really think he was involved, or could this still be a misunderstanding? She looked down; her eyes were tired and sad. Fatigue was apparent on her face and in her posture. She had not slept well in many nights, and the stress of her job was aging her once flawless face. Fine lines of aging started to march across her face like a tiny roadmap. I felt bad for asking her, and I knew the answer before her eyes met mine. A nagging burn deep in the pit of my stomach reminded me that the FBI had its own secrets. Even though she was my friend, she was still an agent, and I needed to remember that.

I was numb as I drove home that night. The time had changed, and by seven thirty, it was black outside. I hated when the time changed, but fall was still one of my favorite times of the year. I loved the crisp feeling in the air and the beautiful colors of the leaves changing. What would I look forward to? The holidays would be here soon; what would they be like? Sadness was weighing me down, and I felt like I could barely hold up my shoulders and my head. I just wanted to cry and forget this was happening. I had thought this nightmare was over; I was moving on. Kayleigh wanted me to carry on with life as normal. She reminded me of my acting skills while in the hospital and wanted me to do this again. I was to act happy, recovered, and like Tripp and I were happily married. This meant at work, at home, and in the bedroom.

The thought of him touching me made me nauseated. If he wanted to kill me, sell me, how was I supposed to fake that love for him? She had clearly overestimated me and my strength. I truly felt like this would break me.

CHAPTER 16

Days turned into weeks, and life went back to its normal rhythm. Daily, I went to work; things seemed easier as time passed. I could almost pretend that the past year of my life had been a dream. Those were good days; I could laugh and joke, take care of my patients. The nurses seemed to want to forget the situation as much as I did; they craved normalcy also. We could once again sit at the desk and talk about our crazy patients, those who were having an affair, and the normal hospital gossip routine.

Then, when I least expected it, the dreams would come. The ones that would seem so real I would awaken in utter terror. Swearing I could smell roses and feel satin sheets on my back. Those nights ended with a hot bath and soothing music. But they seemed to get further apart, which was great.

Sara looked gorgeous with her perfect pregnant figure. Kayleigh had tried to take jobs within an hour travel time to be closer to us. I knew that Tripp was still under investigation, and at first, I tried to look and play the FBI agent myself. I went through his phone, looked in his truck, but never found anything. Over time, I felt like we had made a huge mistake and he was not involved in any way. I pushed the past and my suspicions in the back of my mind. I refused to let this consume me and ruin my life.

The holidays came and seemed more special this year. Aubrey was home; a light sheet of snow covered everything on Christmas Eve. My heart was full of joy and love for my family. The Christmas Eve service at church was wonderful. I loved the smell of the fresh evergreen trees, the lights, and the singing. Kayleigh and I had given Sara a holiday-themed baby shower, and the only time we thought of the past was at that gathering. We remembered the agents and friends Kayleigh had lost; we remembered the women who were gone too soon. But we were so thankful that we were here, celebrating a new little baby.

I was pushed further and further into my land of forgetting, and the gift Tripp gave me made this happen even faster. On Christmas morning, he surprised me with a gift that was beautifully wrapped in metallic green paper. A large red bow was elaborately formed on the top. I knew he had not wrapped this and was intrigued by what could be inside. As I opened the box, I saw a white envelope was inside. The tickets to an all-inclusive five-star resort made me scream in delight. I had always wanted to go to the Dominican Republic, and he had made a dream come true for us. A brochure with pictures of lush green foliage, gorgeous pools, and fancy restaurants made my heart race. He had arranged this wonderful getaway for us and had even arranged for me to be off work. We were going to be leaving New Year's Day. The rest of the day was filled with family gatherings, nieces and nephews, gifts, laughter, and an overall wonderful Christmas.

That night, when Aubrey had gone back to her apartment, I gathered some of my new lotions and bubble bath and took a candlelit bath. I was so happy; the past seemed like a foggy memory that had long past decades ago. I pushed the past trauma further and further into the back recess of my mind. I wanted to be happy and safe, and I was. The future seemed so bright. I could not dwell in the past; I had to move on and take my life back. This is what I was doing, and I was proud of myself. I lay in the jacuzzi with the soft candlelight dancing around me and the scent of lavender filling the air. Pentatonix Christmas played on the speakers, and at that moment, I was in my own little paradise.

The past few weeks, Kayleigh had started dating Dr. Ricardo. There had been no connection to him and Dr. Pierce. I was happy that they had become romantically involved. Of course, he had no idea that she was an FBI agent. She could not tell him this so soon, but she seemed to really like him. Her current assignment had her at a hospital in Winston-Salem, which was only about forty miles from me. The details of the investigation were not divulged to me, but she seemed relaxed and happy. This was the first time I had seen this side of her. Because of my friendship with her, Tripp and I had been invited to a large New Year's Eve party at Dr. Ricardo's house.

He lived in a beautiful area in Lake Norman that was well known for its elaborate homes and lakefront properties.

Mainly physicians and attorneys lived here. Tripp really did not want to go, but I finally persuaded him to go for a little while. With the promise of some good vodka and food, he was more accepting of the idea. Our flight out the next day was not until noon from Charlotte, so we would have plenty of time to finish packing.

I must admit I was nervous, anxious, and a little scared. I had been to work but no social events. Dr. Ricardo was well liked and popular within the community. I knew there would be many physicians who I had not seen since the events that had rocked our small North Carolina town. Hospital management and nurses who were lucky enough to be in his social circle would be attending. I wanted to look amazing and prove to everyone, especially myself, that I was a strong woman who had survived.

A short Sheri-Hill dress is what I decided on. Black and red jewels adorned the entire bodice of the off-the-shoulder dress. I had maintained a weight of 120 pounds, and to help stay in shape and control any hint of panic attacks, I had continued to exercise daily. My hair was placed in an elegant updo by my beautician, and the gorgeous diamond earrings Tripp had given me sparkled and danced when the lights hit them. I looked at myself in the mirror and was pleased. I looked darn good for a woman over forty. Tripp looked sexy as well, and when he saw me, he just stared. Lust and desire danced in his eyes, and my inner core warmed at his expression. He wanted to stay home and ravage me, but I was somewhat successful at keeping his hands off me to get out the door. We laughed and sang all the way to the party. My anxiety about the gathering had long since subsided, and I was excited!

We arrived about thirty minutes late due to horrible holiday traffic, so everyone was aware when we made our entrance. I suspected the people attending were also anxious about seeing me for the first time because the looks of surprise and relief washed over many faces. There were hugs and introductions and champagne. Tripp had always been a social person, never meeting a stranger, so he went on his way bonding and talking ball with other men. After hugs and numerous comments on how I looked, I saw Kayleigh. My eyes had to adjust to the dim lighting, but she was simply breathtaking. I had only seen her in a nursing uniform or casual attire, and tonight was different. Her hair was long but in large, soft curls that framed her face. Her olive-colored skin seemed to glow in the light. She wore a long gold gown that was clinging to her perfect figure and exposed the tops of her essentially perfect breasts. I rushed over to her and pulled her to me. I whispered in her ear how wonderful she looked. She blushed and returned multiple compliments.

I peered into the enormous living room to find the host and thank him for the invite. A beautiful stone fireplace was surrounded by modern Christmas décor. A warm fire was burning, and the tree had remained up for this event. The home was absolutely breathtaking. When I spotted Dr. Ricardo, I was shocked at how he and Kayleigh interacted with one another. I had not seen them out in a social setting, but they seemed like a true couple. His hand rested on the curve of her lower back. He would often kiss her affectionately, and his eyes never stopped surveying the exquisite gold package wrapped in front of him. Kayleigh had confided that they had not been intimate yet, but if they made it through tonight without that changing, I would be shocked.

The night was wonderful with laughing, silly party games, and too much drinking. Stories were told of crazy patients and hospital jokes. Tripp seemed to have a great time and made fast friends with most of the men. Being so close to Charlotte, football was the topic of their conversation. The Panthers were going to the playoffs and were favored to go to the Super Bowl. The Super Bowl party plans were underway. In the middle of the discussion regarding the Panthers' chances of winning, I excused myself to visit the ladies' room. As I walked down the long hallways, I took my time and appreciated the beauty of the home. The smell of pine trees and Christmas still filled the air; music played overhead. Laughter could be heard everywhere within the house.

I got to the end of a hall and realized I was at the library. I love books, so I decided to be nosy and explore. Huge bookshelves lined the walls from the ceiling to the floor, all filled with books. All genres were represented, and I was overcome by the sheer volume of his collection. One wall was dedicated to medicine and what appeared to be his books from med school. The next wall was romance, and then the classic novels and even some first editions on the upper shelves. Elaborate furnishings filled the room with the finest leather chairs and sofas. Multiple glass cases were strategically displayed around the room, encasing precious artifacts. I knew he was an avid sports fan and was not surprised to see a small glass display with a baseball in it. I could not help but smile to myself. I went over to see what was so special about the ball. It looked like a normal ball to me: white, Rawlings; it was signed, but I could not read to whom the signature belonged. There was a gold plaque in the case that read, "Mark McGwire's seventieth home run baseball." Once again amused by the need to place a single ball in a glass case to keep it dust free and preserved made me giggle to myself. The artwork was astounding. I am poorly educated on fine art but am familiar with some of the more famous paintings and current artists. The one piece I really admired was "The Madonna and Child Being Crowned by Two Angels" by Alesso Gozzoli, son of Benozzo Gozzoli. I was aware this most likely was a replica due to the cost of the original piece. The walls were lined with what had to be replicas. I admit, his taste was impeccable. When I saw that the library had a small restroom, I decided to take advantage of my situation. I went in and was touching up my lipstick when I heard someone enter the room. Embarrassed that I was snooping around, I decided to be quiet and wait until they left before exiting.

It only took a moment to realize it was my host and Kayleigh. They were sneaking away from their duties of entertaining and were caught up in a moment of lust. My face flushed as I stood there, not able to mute out the words of sexual advances and teasing. They were both my friends, Kayleigh more like a sister, but I did not need or want to hear this. I was an intruder, a peeping tom! Like a five-year-old throwing a tantrum, I stuck my fingers in my ears. Nothing stopped me from hearing the noises that surrounded me in the small powder room. The smacking of loud, wet kisses; moans of ecstasy; and vulgar words filled the air in the large library. I was uncomfortable in this situation but oddly aroused. Finally, I decided I must exit this room, no matter how awkward or embarrassing; it would be worse if I continued to hide. I decided to flush the toilet and wash my hands, being very loud, much more than I really would have been. They silenced almost immediately and quickly left the room with some laughter. I waited a few more moments and left the room quickly. I rejoined the festivities, and no one even realized my absence.

After the ball drop, the traditional kiss, and New Year toast, Tripp and I decided to head out due to our travel the next day. It was over an hour drive back to our house, and it started in silence. We both had enjoyed our night, and the kiss we had shared at the stroke of midnight had been long and full of hot, fiery passion. As I reached over to hold Tripp's hand, I felt flushed. It wasn't an odd thing for us to hold hands; we still did when we were in the car or walking somewhere. But tonight, it was different. The touch of his hand sent a surge of heat throughout me. I felt it spread onto my breasts like a warm breeze that covered my body and stretched down to my already hot lady parts. I had made sure to purchase some beautiful lingerie from Victoria's Secret, and I was ready for my husband to enjoy it. The open interstate was surprisingly empty. I assumed most people were still at parties. So, in a moment of excitement, I reached back and unzipped my dress. I slipped it off, and in a split second, I was sitting in the front seat of Tripp's Range Rover in my lace bra and panties. He was flushed with excitement, and being a skilled driver, he went to work with his free hand.

To say we barely made it home in one piece is an understatement. We all but made love on I-77 and were practically naked when we busted into the front door. My beautiful dress was in a heap on the floor, along with Tripp's dress pants and tie—I have no idea where his shirt ended up. The night had been so amazing, and tomorrow, our trip would start our New Year off in paradise!

CHAPTER 17

The next morning was filled with last-minute packing and arrangements that are routine when going out of the country. We were both excited, and the thought of my past and the suspicion of Tripp never crossed my mind. This fact alone was a small miracle; I typically did not go an hour without wondering what he was doing and if he was planning to kill me. But the holidays had given me a new perspective. Doubtful that he had anything at all to do with the horrid events, I was determined to live my life and be happy.

The flight was perfect. We were both fatigued from the previous night's events, but the sexual tension was already building. The excitement of a tropical paradise and a much-needed vacation was exhilarating Just as we had landed and were proceeding into the red tape at the airport, my phone vibrated. I quickly looked down to see that I had multiple missed calls from Kayleigh. Of course, my phone had been off during the flight. Once we were finally done and our passports were stamped, I walked over to the restroom to call her back while Tripp awaited our luggage.

Her voice when she answered sent an instant chill down my spine. She demanded to know where I was and what I was doing. Had I forgotten to tell her? I guess I had, with the holidays and since we left so soon the night before; I truly had intended to at the party but had forgotten. It was out of character for her to be so abrupt and stern when speaking to me. Quickly, I explained to her about my wonderful gift and that we had just landed. She was not happy and seemed like something was definitely wrong. This was not the same person I'd witnessed laughing and flirting just a few hours earlier. She explained that she wanted to hear from me twice daily, first thing in the morning and the last at night. She wanted this to be a Snapchat message to prove it was me. My heart was racing by the end of our conversation, but she would not go into detail as to why she was acting so strangely. I kept asking her repeatedly what was wrong, but she would not answer me.

She was probably just upset I had not told her about the trip, so I reassured her once again that everything was fine. I agreed to her demands and politely hung up the phone. My heart was overflowing with love for Tripp, and I refused to believe he was the bad guy. We would have a glorious vacation and put this nightmare of a year far behind us.

Outside the airport awaited the limousine Tripp had arranged; even the ride to paradise was simply luxurious! We sipped expensive champagne, laughed, and kissed like teenagers out on a first date. The resort was simply breathtaking, with elaborate décor and beautiful artwork strategically placed throughout the courtyard and vestibule. Lovely boutiques lined the corridors so visitors could admire the products while walking in the courtyard and to the suites. Quickly, the conversation with Kayleigh had left my mind, and I had the thrill of a new adventure running through my veins.

Entering our suite just accelerated my excitement. The room was something out of a movie. The enormous mahogany doors opened into a lavish foyer. The butler placed our luggage in the large walk-in closets and led us into the main room. The beautiful canopy bed was a Victorian-style piece that was surrounded by the same type of furniture. The bathroom had a double shower that you could fit our entire bathroom from home in. Out on the balcony, which was at least one thousand square feet, there was another cabana bed and an outside hot tub. The view of the Caribbean Sea simply took my breath away. Aqua, blue, and green all mixed with the sunlight shining off the waves. It looked so beautiful that it appeared fake, resembling a painting. After Tripp had tipped the butler, we just stood there and stared at the beauty. I was so thankful to be here, to be alive, and, yes, to be with Tripp.

It only took a few moments and a few soft kisses on the neck before Tripp took me in his arms and threw me on the outdoor cabana bed. At first, I tried to stop him, giggling with embarrassment—we were outside! But he quickly reminded me that we were in the penthouse suite; no one could see us. Then he made quick work of undressing me. The heat of his skin, the salty taste of him and the air, the romantic surroundings made me like a volcano ready to erupt.

The vacation was exactly what we had needed to rekindle our romance and put the past behind us. We enjoyed wonderful dancing and gourmet meals. Dressing in gowns instead of lab coats made me feel young and sexy again. We lay on the beach in the white sands during the day, and our nights were full of shows, cocktails, and a variable sexual buffet.

CHAPTER 18

It wasn't until the fourth afternoon things took a turn. I had called Kayleigh daily, just as she had insisted, and still, she was very odd. She seemed suspicious of why Tripp had planned this trip. I was getting quite upset with her. I refused to let this bring me down, but there was an incident that made me question my own instincts.

There was a weekly "adult foam party" at the pool. The waiters and butlers would spray white clouds of foam all over very intoxicated adults. The pools and the grounds were perfect; then you have a pool full of all ages of adults jumping and screaming. Most of them drunk and acting like teenagers as the foam covered them. I had to admit, I had nothing to drink, but it was so much fun. So silly, messy, but still fun, making you feel young again. Different from the life we had to lead outside of this paradise, like a temporary reprieve from reality. I looked around in wonder of the different people. Some old, some young, various sizes and ethnicities. I laughed to myself as I saw a group of typical rednecks, very country men, hug and fist-bump with other men who looked to be wealthy businessmen. They laughed, joked, hugged, and acted like best friends. I knew that if they had met on a city street, either one would have ignored the other. Totally different lifestyles and economic status, but today, here at this moment, covered in foam and the senses dulled with a variety of mixed alcohol, everyone was brothers.

As I stood and laughed, observed, and also got covered in the white fluffy clouds of foam, the loud music roared all around me. I noticed a beautiful couple coming to join in. It was one of those couples that people notice because they are so beautiful and perfect. He was dark-headed, looked to be of Arabic descent. A small, manicured beard and mustache accented his sharp jawline. He was very masculine, with sculpted shoulders and arms. A six-pack set of abdominal muscles to let everyone know he worked hard on his flawless physique. He was leading an exquisite dark-headed lady by the hand. She had a very small bikini on that made me jealous of her youth and beauty. She was adorned with large gold earrings, gold diamond bracelets, and her perfect abdomen was adorned with a diamond ring. The diamond on her left hand looked to be at least a four-karat if not more. He was all smiles as he led her down the narrow path in front of the cabana beds, weaving in and out of the palm trees. The crowd peered up at them; I think everyone noticed. I wondered if he came in late just to make the entrance. If this was his plan, it worked. All eyes were on them. The women screamed, and the men let out some type of low, growling cheer. Quite primitive, really, but he loved it. He waved and did a fist pump in the air.

I wondered if I was the only one to notice that she never looked up. Her dark eyes were down the whole time, I thought initially to try to keep her balance and maneuver not falling into the pool. But it seemed like when they finally reached the cabana bed he felt suitable, she remained melancholy. He was joking and laughing with every testosterone-filled man he passed, still pulling her along like a child. Not a single smile crossed her perfect face. Her full, pouty lips, painted a pale pink that perfectly matched her expensive-appearing swimsuit, never moved in the slightest. He quickly threw his towel down and plunged into the pool. Men and women were naturally drawn to him, just like in the real world, I assumed. But she just sat on the end of the chair. She carefully placed her bag on the table and with her perfect posture sat there, not even offering to get involved in the action taking place. He never spoke to her, never addressed her, and he was quickly engulfed in the sea of foam and never looked back at her. I was so intrigued by her. Not just her beauty, but the oddity of the situation. I was aware that this culture treated women differently, and I was only assuming his Arabic descent at first, but after hearing him speak, I was positive. I glanced around to see where Tripp had disappeared to and discovered he was having a blast playing a game at the other end of the pool with the good ole country boys from Texas.

I decided I'd had enough of hot, sweaty, drunk bodies bumping up against me. Most of them smelled of body odor and booze mixed with the sweet smell of the foam; I was getting nauseated.

I got out, walked over to the cabana bed we had placed our bag on, and decided to bake my winter-white skin in the sun. The bed I was stretched out upon was perpendicular to the mystery lady's bed, and my eyes seemed to be drawn to her. I knew I shouldn't stare, but I just couldn't help myself. Her perfect olive skin seemed to glow in the sunlight. She eventually decided to lie back and recline on the cabana bed, I assumed to soak up some sun. I felt like a weirdo staring at her, so I decided to read my book. This was a good thought but short-lived because the blaring music made it hard to focus, and I found myself reading the same sentence over and over. Feeling like I was going to self-combust due to the heat, I wrapped my sarong around my waist and went to the bar. As I strolled by the bed, I could not help but look down at the beautiful young lady.

Immediately, I felt my heart stop, but my pulse bounded in my head louder than the music playing around me. Despite sweating, a cold feeling ran throughout my veins, and nausea quickly followed. For a moment, I wondered if I were having a heat stroke. Was I just too hot? Then I remembered this feeling—it was a panic attack. It had been so long since I'd had one that I had forgotten how horrible it was. My brain took longer to catch up to my body, it seemed, because it took a few moments for me to register why this one had started from nowhere. I had completely frozen, like a sick, voyeuristic woman just staring down at her. I could not move; I was screaming in my head to move and stop looking like a freak, but I could not. Since I was blocking her sunlight, she eventually opened her eyes and sat up. She slowly pulled off her Versace sunglasses and made eye contact with me. We stared at each other; she looked at me at first with irritation, but as she evaluated me with her eyes, surveying me up and down, her expression changed. As she came to my abdomen, right above my sarong, she stopped. Her eyes changed from hardness to fear and pity. Then I knew. I saw her incision on her right upper abdomen, and I knew what had caused my body to once again betray me without warning.

CHAPTER 19

Women have an uncanny way of communicating without saying a word. Sometimes it's a nod, a look, or a gesture, and in this situation, all it took was the movement of her eyes toward the pool. I knew quickly to act like I had dropped something, pick it up, and move away. As I turned from her, trying not to look suspicious, my heart was racing so badly I feared I would pass out at any time. The feeling that the men in the pool were all staring at us, that I had been noticed, was making the panic worsen with each stride toward the bar. When I arrived and found a stool, I tried to nonchalantly look back. Of course, no one cared about what I was doing. The foam was pouring out, the booze continued to flow, and drunk bodies continued to jump and scream in the pool. All eyes were not on me, and I took a big sigh of relief as I tried to see where the mystery lady had gotten to. I knew she had also gotten up but was not behind me when I made it to the bar.

I asked for the signature drink, which was like an orange dream popsicle with alcohol in it. As I awaited the bartender to get done blending the tropical concoction, another butler approached me and handed me a small note, tightly folded. He discreetly placed it in my hand and quickly disappeared. I knew not to open it right there, so I acted like it never happened. Quickly surveying my surroundings, it seemed that no one was even paying attention to me. When my orange delight arrived, I took a long, hard drink and slowly made my way back to our cabana bed. I tried to locate Tripp, but really everyone by this point was covered in foam, and I could not tell my husband apart from the other twenty-five or so men acting like drunken maniacs.

Finally, the lady arrived back at her bed, never even letting her eyes drift toward me. She kept her eyes down, adjusted her towel and sunglasses, and resumed her previous position. Briefly, her companion walked over to her and whisper something in her ear. His hand caressed at first her thigh and abdomen, but very quickly, in one fast motion, he grabbed her chin as he spoke. He placed a forceful kiss on her full lips and walked away. The whole exchange was fast, and no one would have noticed that it was awkward, but I was watching, and I knew.

After what seemed like hours, my intoxicated spouse emerged from his sea of foam, laughing and singing off-key to the Justin Bieber hit "Despacito." This had become his favorite song not only because it was number one on the charts right now, but because they played it constantly!

I hurriedly got him back to the penthouse suite, knowing he would quickly be snoring as soon as his head hit the bed. An afternoon nap was common, and he would take a good two-hour siesta before dinner. When my task at hand was finished, and he was snoring like a loud grizzly during hibernation, I ran my bubble bath. Also, my afternoon ritual: to have a bath and read. But today it would not be my typical suspense thriller; it would be my note.

I wanted to do nothing to draw suspicion to myself because the very ugly monster in my head was running crazy with thoughts of deception. How could it be a coincidence that we were at the same resort as another victim?

The large jacuzzi tub filled, and I poured the upscale bath salts in. Soon, the room was filled with the aroma of tropical flowers. I could hear the rhythmic cadence of Tripp's snoring and placed the note within my book. I was not sure why I was so overly cautious; he was clearly in an alcohol-induced coma with no sign of regaining consciousness within the next hour. But deep within me, I felt the horrible feeling that had been suppressed for so long and went into defense mode. With the warm water surrounding my sunburned body, I opened the note. Quickly, chills covered me as I read the perfectly written tiny words.

I know you, as you know me. We are sisters in a very special family. I would love to meet you and talk. Discretion is imperative. I have a spa appointment at 2:00 p.m. tomorrow. Please join me. The spa is women only.

She was smart in not saying too much but saying just enough to let me know I was right, and we had been in the same situation. My mind raced; I needed to figure out if she had been with me or if she was from a different auction. I adjusted my pillow, lay back into the warm water, took slow, deep breaths, and tried to relax. The strong smell of the perfumed salts floated in the air, and I felt my tense muscles relax. The memories of those terrible events had been pushed deep into the back recesses of my mind, and I hated to bring them back. But I needed to; I needed to remember those women, the faces. The problem was that I did not see a lot of the faces, only the bodies of some of the victims. I pressed on, pushing my subconscious to the limit. I went back to the time in the auction, the smell of the roses and feel of the sheets, sounds of soft music filling the air. I tried to recall each face, but I did not remember seeing the lady. She had such distinct features, and from my memory, I did not recall her at all.

Time must have gone faster than it seemed because I was snapped out of my trance by Tripp touching my arm. The loud scream that erupted from me made him jump, and he looked quite shocked by my state of anxiety. Asking me if I was all right, he reached down to pick up my book. I quickly recovered and reassured him that I had dozed off and was fine. I felt sure he had not seen the little piece of paper and continued in my soothing bath for little longer, trying to gather my thoughts. I wasn't sure if I should just go or if I should talk to Kaleigh first. I knew how she would react; she would immediately accuse Tripp of being involved again. I wasn't sure if he was or was not, but I did not want to jump to that assumption yet. I was not ready to fall back into that life of suspicion again. I thought that was over, that we had moved past it. Tears streamed down my cheeks, and I began to weep before I had even realized it.

My heart broke for the normal life I used to have, the simple life of going to work and coming home. The weekends of cleaning the house and lying by the pool. Aubrey in college and Tripp at work, cookouts and family gatherings. Nothing would ever be the same. These men had taken my life from me. But the lingering question was creeping back into my mind: was my own husband involved in this? I could not help but to think how odd it was that he had arranged this trip, and I saw a woman who had been at an auction like myself. It seemed too much of a coincidence to me. Maybe Kayleigh knew more about this than she had revealed. I had known something was not right since her call. Trying to decide how to handle this was almost overwhelming. I wanted to crawl into a shell like a turtle and hide from this whole nightmare. I rested there in my porcelain refuge for a little while longer, then decided to get out. I needed to get myself pulled together and get a plan.

Tripp had showered and was dressing for dinner when I finally came out of the protection of my liquid relaxation. I had flushed the note down the toilet and made sure he would never see it just in case he was involved. As I dried my long hair and applied a thin coat of makeup, I decided to not make Kayleigh aware yet of what was going on. At dinner, I started to formulate a plan of action.

The Italian restaurant was our choice that night. It was a beautiful restaurant decorated with lavish couches, and paintings covered the walls. A huge mural surrounded the entirety of the back wall where we were seated. Tripp looked handsome in his tuxedo, and I felt a tug of sadness and despair, not knowing if secretly he was involved. But I had to pull out the actress in me once again and act like nothing was wrong. We laughed and flirted and discussed the wonderful time we'd had on this trip. This was when I decided to tell him I had scheduled a spa treatment for myself. I get regular massages and enjoy going to the spa, so he was not at all suspicious. Planning to go to the casino himself, he was happy to be away from me for a few hours. The rest of the night ended like all the others, sitting on the balcony, drinking a glass of wine. I was able to fake some stomach issues and excused myself early.

My night was not a restful one. I had dreams of tight boxes and being buried alive. My mind traveled back in my sleep to the dark, tight spaces in the hospital, and the fear I had suppressed for months came back that night. Like a dark enemy, the fear crept its way in my dreams and in my mind. It all came back to me, the emotions and the panic. When I woke up, the sweat was beaded all over my sunburned skin; the expensive Egyptian sheets were damp. I did not feel refreshed like the previous mornings. I felt anxious with my insides nervous and jumpy.

Restful nights were a luxury of my past, I would soon come to realize.

CHAPTER 20

The spa was located at the sister resort next door, and it was three stories of pampering fit for a queen. The weather was gorgeous, and the walk along the perfectly manicured paths made me feel better and less on edge. After the horrible night, I needed to relax and calm down. I had spent the morning out on the beach sipping a variety of mixed drinks and felt much better, but this was what I needed. A great massage and getting some answers would put my mind at ease.

The waiting area was full of women, all excited and ready for their various treatments. This was a five-star spa and offered multiple services and packages. I did not see the mystery lady immediately, but as I signed in at the desk, I could see into the hot springs room. This was a huge heated indoor pool that was made to look like an outdoor paradise of hot springs. Large rocks lined the walls with a beautiful waterfall in the middle. The water was advertised to have minerals and dead sea salts to rejuvenate and replenish your skin. Women were lying in various areas of the rocked oasis, some in swimsuits, many naked. This spa was strictly for female use only, so clothing was optional. The flowers and tropical plants were placed in every open space possible, and I could not help but be utterly shocked by this breathtaking beauty.

Then I saw her—just as I signed my name on my receipt, my eye was drawn to a far corner. The light was dim in this area, and I knew why she had chosen it. If a person were not really looking, you would not notice the area at all. I did not act any differently and reviewed my spa schedule. I had an hour in the hot springs before the massage, then sauna time. Going to the dressing room, I found the locker I had been assigned and changed. Being naked was not in my comfort zone, so, putting on my suit and robe, I headed toward the area. I went slowly, sipping the expensive champagne I had been handed at check-in. I pretended to admire the flowers and acted like I had no reason or urgency to talk to the woman I was headed toward.

Finally arriving by her side, I sat, not speaking a word. As I had walked toward her, I had once again admired her beauty. She was simply astounding, with flawless skin and hair. She was very aware of her own flawless physique and was nude rather than clothed. Her perfectly perky breasts were at full attention with the slight chill in the air. The steam from the springs had caused some small droplets of condensation to sit sensually in her cleavage.

After a few moments had passed, she spoke in a low, throaty voice. "I am glad you decided to join me." I didn't respond verbally but with a subtle nod, so she continued. "We have much to discuss, and I know time is of the essence, for we cannot communicate outside of the safety of this spa, and even here, I am hesitant." I noted an undertone of anxiety in her voice. She was clearly very nervous to be here with me.

Not knowing exactly where to start, I introduced myself. "My name is Layla Matthews. I am from the United States, and I live in North Carolina."

Her eyes remained fixed ahead, looking out into the oasis full of women. The picture resembled some type of artist's depiction of women bathing at a medieval volcano in ancient times. I could not help but be amused. She nodded at my introduction and explained that her name was Somaya Ahseed "*now.*" The way she said it instantly let me know that this was not the name she'd had previously. She did not have the same Arabic accent her spouse had. Hers was definitely American, and I could detect a northern undertone. She explained that she'd lived in Dubai for the past two years. She kept her voice low and even; I could tell she had put a lot of thought into what she needed to say during our short amount of time together. Before living in Dubai, she was from Philadelphia and was twenty-four years old. At the age of twenty-two, she had graduated from Temple University with a degree in broadcast journalism. She was not sure how it had happened, but she had essentially awakened after being abducted and found herself in the United Arab Emirates. She had become the property of a wealthy man who lived there. For the first few months, she was kept captive and isolated from everyone else and told over and over that she was his property now and would never leave. Once a strong-willed, independent young woman start-ing her career in journalism, the task of brainwashing her was not easy for her capturers. Finally realizing that she would not ever be able to leave, resigned to her new life, a new identity, and knowing that she would never be free, she began to play the part. She was always monitored by her husband or his staff. This was ironically the first trip they had taken that his staff had not been with her and the first time she had been truly alone in the past two years.

At one point, she paused cautiously when the waitress en-quired if we needed more refreshments. Acting very casual, she rhythmically changed the conversation to fashion and never lost her tempo. If the waitress had been sent to check up on her, she would never suspect a thing. Sensing her nervous ten-sion, I stretched as to appear bored with the conversation and stood up. I stepped off the small rock perch we had been lying on and dipped down into the water. The hot, salty water felt amazing, and the tension that had slowly crept into my back and neck released. Waiting for a few moments, making sure no one was watching us, she rolled over and began to pick back up with her story.

She was scared at first and had no way of knowing what had happened to her. No access to Internet or phones, so she could not contact anyone at all. Eventually, she was shown her obituary and informed that everyone she had known in the USA thought she was dead, and if she ever tried to contact them, they would all die. Knowing her captor was a dangerous and powerful man, she knew he would keep his promise. She had no other option but to become the submissive wife and slave he desired.

"I have no idea what has happened to me, why I ended up there, but I do know that the scars on my body were not there before. Until I saw you and saw the same scars on your body, I thought I was the only one." She explained to me that she wanted to grab me, scream, and run, but over the past two years, she had learned how to control any emotions she felt. She was not allowed to speak without being spoken to; her opinion did not matter. She was to keep her appearance flawless and be available to fulfill any desire of her spouse at all times. If she did not submit to these demands, she was punished. Never scarred but beaten, starved for days, and many more horrible punishments were inflicted upon her. She was hopeful that I could provide answers to what had happened to her and how she had been declared dead when she knew she had not died. Knowing that my massage time was quickly approaching, I knew I could not even touch the surface of what had happened to her. I did not know how she'd gotten to the auction, but she obviously had been purchased at an event much like the one I was at.

I could see her chest rapidly rise and fall as the clock ran down on our time together. Knowing that typical spas are on a very tight schedule, we would both be done in exactly ninety minutes. I told her to meet me in the sauna, and we could continue. She nodded to me, and I got out of the warm, soothing liquid just as my name was called. I was practically in a fog as I went up the marble staircase to the rooms where the massages were done.

Unable to really enjoy the experience, I used this time to get my thoughts together. I knew the time I would have in the sauna would be short and I would not be able to tell her all the details. I knew she had rehearsed the information relayed to me, giving me important pieces on who she was. I needed to do the same for her in what little time I had. When I was finished and was dressing, I grabbed my cell and quickly messaged Kayleigh. I knew I needed to update her ASAP. *Need to talk as soon as possible! Urgent, but don't panic. I am fine, but something has happened. Text me the best time to call!*

Hurrying to the sauna, I looked for my new acquaintance. This was not the typical small box with steam; it was a huge room with bamboo benches lining the walls. A large pit of hot lava rocks filled the room with a steady fog of steam. Glistening bodies were laid out on the benches, and in here, no one was dressed. So, I thought, *What the heck?* and disrobed. Somewhat self-consciously, I tried to adjust my eyes and find Somaya. Hearing her clear her throat, I was able to locate her and swiftly went to her side. I laid myself the opposite way on the bench, and we were essentially face to face. The steam was so thick we did not have to act like we weren't talking, and the room was loud with the sound of the constant sizzling steam and the low hum of music.

Quickly, I explained that there was a group of physicians and businessmen who had made a sick franchise of selling women, some for organs and others into sexual slavery, a "body auction." She had obviously been purchased to marry this man. I explained how I had been given the medication to paralyze me, and due to a malfunction, I was able to escape. She listened and never changed her expression. She was lying perfectly motionless on the bench, her long, black hair billowed to the side, and her eyes remained closed the entire time I spoke. My words were quick and deliberate. I let her know that the FBI had always felt that this was a much larger operation; the investigation had been ongoing but was almost impossible due to the fake deaths. Knowing this would most likely be the last time we could talk, I wanted her real name. Planning to give Kaleigh the information, I wanted to find out all I could in what little time we had left.

That was the first time I saw a small tear escape the side of her eye. Her perfectly shaped mouth quivered with emotion that was smoldering underneath, being held tightly inside of her. Like a quiet volcano, her core must have felt like lava waiting to escape its shell. I could not imagine how she felt hearing the things I had just relayed to her. It literally took me months to be able to deal with what happened, and I had just let it flow from my mouth like it was a casual happening. Not rushing her, I waited for her to respond. She repeatedly swallowed like you do when trying to hold in a sob, then finally, in a small, meek voice, she said, "My name was Rhonda Asad."

"I think he chose me because of my Arabic descent. He has mentioned that he would never marry a woman who was not Muslim. I was born in America, but my mother and father are both Egyptian. He could not find a suitable wife, so he has told me many times I was 'handpicked by ALLAH' to be his wife." She went on to explain that he knew many details about her family, appearing as though he had researched her. My mind raced on how she'd been chosen for the auction, but there was no time for details at this moment. She rapidly fired off the names of her father and mother and was getting into more details when a tall, slender woman came up to us. Startled by her appearance out of the fog, she spoke to Rhonda in a somewhat condescending tone. "Mrs. Ahseed, I am sorry to interrupt you, but your sauna time is complete and your husband requests for you to meet him out front shortly."

I immediately felt a hot rage well up inside me, and I sat up and started to object when she softly touched my hand and shook her head. Her dark eyes met mine, and even though she didn't say a word, her look spoke volumes to me. Grateful for the steam and sweat that was constantly running down my face, I knew the lady would not notice the tears that had begun to pour from my eyes. Pain surged through me. How could I let her leave? I had to help her; I had to save her! I had been saved, and I had left those other women behind to be taken. So many times, I had blamed myself and wondered what happened to them, and now I knew somewhere they were just like Rhonda, scared and not knowing what had happened to them.

Watching her walk away, I was shocked by her mannerisms. She stood, tall and proud, and seemed to literally remove the sorrow from moments ago, like a cloak being removed. With all the elegance of any of the wealthy women surrounding us, she sauntered out of the sauna, never looking back. As I looked down in awe, I saw something glimmer like a light breaking through the fog. A small diamond earring was lying in the place where her head had just been. I jumped up just as the door shut but stopped her in time. Pretending to return a piece of jewelry accidentally found, I placed it in her hand. Thanking me, she hugged me, and quickly I whispered in her ear, "I will find you. I promise, I will save you!" Without a word or even a sign that I had spoken, she was gone.

CHAPTER 21

The next few days of our trip were spent relaxing. I felt like my head was in the clouds most of the time. Everywhere we went, I looked nonstop for Rhonda. I wanted to see her so badly. I knew I could not talk to her, but just seeing her would give me some semblance of comfort. But this did not happen; I never saw her again after leaving the sauna.

I had called Kayleigh that night after dinner, when Tripp had gone to get a drink at the bar. Knowing I had plenty of time because the football game was on, I was able to give her details of the encounter. She listened intently, and I could tell she was taking mental notes like she always did. Reassuring me, she said she would start investigating ASAP. When we hung up, I called Aubrey. I was so proud of my daughter. Who would have ever thought she would be training to be an FBI agent? I repeated to her all the things I had just told Kayleigh, leaving out my concerns about Tripp's involvement. We had never really discussed that, and I had no idea how to approach it, but now wasn't the time. Both ladies agreed to start a full probe into Rhonda's story, and I felt somewhat better about the situation.

The next thing on my mind was getting home. It was amazing that a few short days ago, this horrible event had been far behind me. Now rearing its ugly head, I was staring it in the face once again. Not knowing who to trust and being on guard all the time made me miserable. The flight and ride home were uneventful, with Tripp sensing my distance. I tried to play it off as traveler's fatigue and sadness that we were home. He was equally tired and seemed content with my excuses.

We arrived at home late in the evening, and Aubrey was there waiting. I was anxious to see her but somewhat worried she would bring up Rhonda. Since I was not able to discuss the suspicions we had about Tripp, she may bring up the topic. But thankfully, she never mentioned it. We told her about the trip and showed her a few pictures, and she decided to spend the night. I had very little in the house to eat, but we put some things together and had a nice late dinner. I had taken the day off, as I typically did after vacation, to recover, but Tripp had to work. Hoping to catch up more with Aubrey in the morning, I finally was able to sleep more peacefully with her in the house.

Being able to sleep in my own bed and shower in my house left me feeling refreshed and renewed the next morning. Shocked to hear the doorbell chime early, I grabbed my coffee and went to see who it was. Kayleigh was a sight for sore eyes, as the saying goes. I almost dropped my coffee when she hugged me, and out of nowhere, I started to weep. Drives me crazy how my emotions have a tendency to give me no warning anymore. One moment I am fine, and then the next, I am a blubbering fool. We just stood there, embraced tightly, and I had no intention of letting go until I heard Aubrey walk into the foyer. Embarrassed by my show of emotion, I let Kayleigh out of the death grip. We all went into the kitchen and started opening the bag of bagels she had brought with her. No one spoke until we had our coffees and bagels and were seated in the breakfast nook.

I was quickly updated on what little they were able to discover about Rhonda. She had lived in Philadelphia and, as she had told me, attended Temple University. Her father was a well-known physician who was Egyptian that had come to the US to finish his medical training when he was in his early twenties. This was when he had met her mother, also Egyptian but born in the US. She had a younger brother who was still in college at Temple. They had no idea how she'd been placed in the auction yet, but I was impressed they had this much in such a small amount of time. Rhonda was just listed as deceased, and the details of that were more difficult to find out.

They did have some articles and pictures of her, and seeing them made me instantly start tearing up. She'd been a promising student in the journalism program, had an internship at CBS, and was ultimately working for CNN when she died. The article talked about how energetic and promising she was, with multiple attributes to her young life cut too short by tragedy. We needed to know all the details of her death, where and how this had happened. Meeting her had sparked a fire under the FBI. Knowing this was a much larger crime ring but not being able to get any leads for months had made the investigation somewhat stale, so Kayleigh and Aubrey were ecstatic.

I did not feel excited for the same reason. Don't get me wrong—I wanted everyone on earth involved in this to be put in jail, but I only wanted to get Rhonda. I needed her to be safe. I was sitting there in my silk robe and eating a bagel. I could come and go as I pleased, but she was being held captive. Focusing on anything else was impossible for me at this point.

Kayleigh and Aubrey informed me that they were going to Philadelphia to meet with her brother to get some details. Of course, I wanted to go, but they did not seem too excited about the idea. Knowing I needed to work the next day, I did not put up a big fight. When Aubrey finally excused herself to shower, I had time alone with Kayleigh. Immediately, I wanted to know what else she knew; it was clear she was hiding something because nothing about Tripp was even mentioned. She proceeded to explain after the New Year's party, she ended up spending the night. I wanted the dirty details, but now was not the time. Her expression was serious and stern as she talked. She told me that when Dr. Ricardo had gone out for breakfast the next morning, she went to the library to find something to read. She accidentally discovered a photo album and, out of curiosity, looked through it. The album was full of pictures of fishing trips and groups of men in various locations. Some hunting boar on a huge plantation in Georgia, others on a yacht trophy fishing. I still wondered what this had to do with her calling me and acting so odd about my trip, and she finally got to the real issue. In one of the sections, there were pictures of a group of men at a resort, a five-star resort in the Dominican Republic. The place was gorgeous, and she could not help but want to go there sometime. After a night of romance and her budding feelings for Dr. Ricardo, she imagined a trip there with him someday. When he returned, she didn't hide that she had looked at the album, and of course, he didn't mind. She enquired about the resort. He told her the name and explained that it had been a group of physicians he had worked with and a few drug reps.

None of this was surprising; drug companies many years ago could pay for trips and host physicians and, in some cases, their families. The laws have changed now, and this is no longer allowed, but sometimes favors are still played. She recognized a few of the men from working at the hospital, but nothing was odd to her at first. Later that morning, she had checked in with headquarters, where she had spoken to Aubrey. This is how she learned of the vacation Tripp had surprised me with. When she heard the location and the name of the resort, she got somewhat suspicious, thinking that was an odd coincidence. Since Dr. Ricardo was in the shower, she went back to the library and took the book out, hiding the album in her car. Finally, they gave their goodbyes, and she quickly went to the office to really investigate the album.

In the privacy of her office, she was able to look at all pictures and start a log of the men. The different locations, names, and dates were logged. Discovering that the resort Tripp had taken me to was the exact one in the photo made her blood turn to ice. What made things worse was the men in the photo.

One of them looked familiar to her. At the initial auction, some of the men did not return for the sale. Therefore, they had not been arrested. Most of the buyers had been arrested due to the logs and financial information kept, but not all of the physicians were found. With Kayleigh's memory being so photographic, she remembered a dark-headed man. He had been one of the men we had seen in the OR that night helping with the testing they were doing on Sara. When she told me this, I tried to think back to that night, in that dark space watching them do those horrible things to my friend. I closed my eyes while she spoke and took myself back to that night. I looked at the faces one by one, and I did recall one man who was in that OR, but I did not remember seeing him again. There had been so many faces and so much drowsiness from medications, I had not even given that another thought.

When Kayleigh discovered this, she was concerned. We had not been able to prove Tripp had been involved, but the suspicions had been there for the both of us. She asked me if I knew how Tripp had decided on that specific resort, but of course, I had no idea. I had assumed he had googled it and done some research. I did not ask—I had no reason to; it was a Christmas gift.

In doing more extensive research, she discovered the physician was a surgeon from Miami. He was an orthopedic surgeon who had gotten into some trouble with the medical board for doing excessive surgical procedures. He also had been accused of sexual misconduct with a few patients; ultimately, his license to practice was suspended. It was still inactive, and his location was currently unknown. I was trying to piece things together and decide how Tripp could have possibly picked the same resort these men had been to—and how would I find out?

By the time Kaleigh had updated me on what they had discovered, Aubrey was out of the shower, and it was time to say our goodbyes. They were planning on leaving in the late afternoon for Philadelphia, and I needed to unpack and clean before I went back to work the next day. As I hugged my sweet, beautiful daughter goodbye, I had an eerie feeling come over me, one like something bad was about to happen. I did not want to let her go. I had the same feeling as I said goodbye to Kayleigh. Why did I feel like this was a last goodbye? I shook this off. I mean, they were just going to talk to Rhonda's brother—how dangerous was that? So, I made myself busy washing clothes and trying to put my crazy suspicions out of my mind. I had the assignment to also look through Tripp's computer and snoop his search engine to try to find some clues.

As the day went on and I got the work around the house done, I finally sat down to look at Tripp's laptop. I started at his searches, and just as I thought, he had googled multiple resorts. Then I went into his emails and researched back to around October, when I assumed he'd booked the trip. What was odd was that he had multiple emails to and from Dr. Ricardo. I didn't even know they communicated with each other. I went back as far as I could go and found when they started. It was right after I had come home. He had emailed Tripp to see how I was doing, and they had communicated sporadically throughout the months. Then I found what I was looking for. Tripp had told him that he was thinking about taking me away as a surprise and asked if he recommended any resorts. Of course, this was the resort Dr. Ricardo suggested. *That's innocent enough*, I thought. He had been there, and it was probably a coincidence that they had been there on a drug rep trip with one of the psychos. Dr. Ricardo had no idea what was going on, and that trip had been a few years ago anyway. Finding this made me feel much better because I could reassure Kayleigh that Tripp was not involved and there was nothing sinister about our trip. But in the back of my mind, I knew it was too much of a coincidence that Rhonda was there also. So, in my typical way of dealing, I shoved it in the back of my mind and prepared dinner.

The afternoon was normal, dinner and TV. I could tell the distance that had disappeared once was back between Tripp and me. The fact is, I knew all too well it was my fault. I just could not face him, I could not help but still think he was involved. So, I went to bed with my mind wondering once again.

CHAPTER 22

ubrey and Kayleigh had no idea what they would find when they went to speak to Rhonda's brother. They could not tell him the reason they were there and why they would be asking about his deceased sister. They decided on the plane to present themselves as interns from a local newspaper who wanted to do an article on her. She had been a great student at Temple, graduated with honors, and died before her amazing career started. This was going to be one of Aubrey's first assignments, and she was excited and nervous beyond words. Her attire was "nerdier," as she described it, to play the part, and Kayleigh had to get a more "youthful" outfit than she was accustomed to.

Rhonda's brother was living in a studio apartment. He was still in college, attending Temple and hoping to go to medical school, following in his father's footsteps. When they had contacted him about the interview, he was excited about getting to honor his sister's memory.

Kayleigh was calm and cool, and Aubrey could see that she had done this many times before. She introduced them and thanked him for helping them get the information they needed on his sister's life, which had been taken so prematurely.

Ahmed was tall, dark-headed, and strikingly handsome. Aubrey's heart was already beating out of her chest, and the sight of him made it go even faster. She just stood there and looked up at his physique, which was gorgeous. His dark, wavy hair; sharp, angular jawline; and tiny, manicured mustache were almost making her dizzy. Trying to make sure her mouth was not hanging open, she was having a hard time even saying hello to him. Seeing that she was smitten, Kayleigh took over and did all the talking at first.

More than enthusiastic to discuss his sister with the "reporters," he welcomed them in. His small but very well-decorated apartment was impressive to them both. After the normal introductions and pleasantries had taken place, the interview began. They quickly got to the point of why they were there, to find out more about Rhonda. He explained what a beautiful, vibrant young lady she had been. Tears spilled over his dark, mesmerizing eyes more than once. He described what a great student she had been, and he was convinced she would have had an amazing and successful career in journalism. He spoke of her with such love and admiration they both were deeply touched. Aubrey had an internal struggle about this situation early in the interview., knowing she was not really dead. But the main thing they needed to know was how she'd been discovered by the brokers to be used in the body auction.

At one point, when he politely offered them refreshments, they decided to try to shift the questions. Aubrey finally got the courage to speak, and she started with the most difficult questions: what had happened to his young sister? He started by telling about his mother. Once again, while talking, his eyes almost glazed over as he took his mind back to remember his mother. Aubrey almost started to cry when the tears rolled down his perfectly shaped cheeks. When he was young, his father had moved away to North Carolina to practice medicine. His mother had essentially raised the two of them. She had been their best friend, a tough disciplinarian who pushed them to excel in school; at the same time, she was loving and understanding. They both felt like she was their best friend as well as the best mother in the world. They were devastated to learn she had terminal cancer and did not survive over two years after her diagnosis. He gave them a family picture while he described her to them. She was equally as breathtaking as her children. She had a petite frame with strong Middle Eastern features. Her hair was shining like a black pearl in the picture. She was exquisite and like a beautiful flower had withered quickly from the monstrous disease she had been afflicted with.

He went on to tell them how Rhonda was almost destroyed by the loss of her mother. She had stayed at the hospital by her side almost non-stop. There was one night toward the end that Rhonda had been extremely fatigued—she had not eaten or slept in days and almost passed out. This was when she met a physician who became friends with her. He was worried about her and took a special interest in her. He made her promise that she would get a checkup and follow up with him after the arrangements were made and their mother had been laid to rest.

Already, Kayleigh and Aubrey were putting the pieces together. Trying to stay calm, they listened intently and made notes. He went on to explain that Rhonda seemed depressed and declined physically very quickly. He tried to encourage her and get her therapy, but nothing seemed to bring her out of the fog she was in. She had lab work and some testing, and their father came and tried to help all he could. But their mother had been the love of his life, and he too was broken-hearted and provided little comfort for his daughter. Finally, a diagnosis was given to her, not just depression but a condition called Takotsubo cardiomyopathy or "broken heart syndrome." It was a condition that is more common in women and can occur after they have had a severe physical or emotional stressor. Typically, the patients will improve over time, and she was given encouragement and some medications.

She did not improve, and while he had been on a trip with some college friends, Ahmed got the call that she had gone into the ER after passing out again and ultimately had a cardiac arrest. He was told that her weakened heart could not recover, and she had expired. He, of course, was devastated and never had any reason to question things.

Their father had completely lost his will to live after this. His wife had been the love of his life, and now, with his daughter's passing, it was too much to withstand. He stopped practicing medicine, moved to Florida, and was a recluse.

Both ladies could see the emotional torture this was placing on him. To think he was all alone and he had no idea the truth. His father, who was a renowned physician and had a reputation for being a brilliant man, had stopped doing what he loved. How many lives had been ruined by this horrible business of death?

Aubrey wanted to vomit the truth right then and there, but she knew she had to hold back for now. When they left, she was trembling all over, angry and torn that they could not reveal the truth and give him peace. She had felt so close to him, most likely due to the fact they were the same age and he was also gorgeous. Kayleigh, being older and more experienced, kept a calm demeanor and reassured Aubrey. The next step was to go to the hospital and see what records they could get. During the interview, they asked if he could remember the names of the physicians that treated Rhonda, but he could not and seemed to get a little suspicious with that line of questioning. Quickly changing the plan, they went to the hospital where Rhonda's mother had been treated.

Taking a moment to get changed, they put on classy business suits and fake Joint Commission nametags. With the proper documentation, they put on the serious game faces and went into the administration of the Mother of Mercy Medical Center.

CHAPTER 23

oint Commission walking into a hospital, or any healthcare facility for that matter, sends a surge of terror throughout the halls. The nurses run into patient rooms and hide; administration starts to send secret emergency messages to the department heads. They panic because this organization can cause serious damage to a facility, and they are a truly feared branch of the healthcare hierarchy. It was not difficult for the FBI to get the clearance they needed and with the proper documents, *all* hospital records were at their disposal. The hospital administrator was, of course, upset about this surprise visit. The Joint Commission can come unannounced, but it is not very common. A few days' warning is typical but not mandatory.

Kayleigh could not help but to laugh to herself, remembering what it was like to be on the other end of a Joint Commission surveyor question. She was enjoying this on many levels but was anxious about reviewing the records from the night Rhonda came in. After the awkwardness of fake pleasantries, they were placed in a conference room with laptops, passcodes, and ice waters. The reception was anything but warm, but they had what they needed.

Aubrey had never worked in the medical field and had no idea what to do or what she was looking at. Kayleigh put her to work looking up the hospital's physician directory. She was going to see if any of the physicians were the ones we had encountered. After a few moments, Kayleigh had the records, and they were looking all the names of the treating physicians up on the directory.

Minutes turned quickly to hours, and as the time built, so did the tension among the two women. Nothing was sticking out as suspicious at all. None of the physicians crossed referenced with the ones at our auction. None of them had even been employed in the same state. Knowing that Dr. Pierce had practiced medicine under many different names kept the hope of finding something alive. They changed the focus to the medical records of Rhonda's mother. All physicians who had been on her case were recorded, and while Kayleigh read the lengthy medical record, she would call out the name of every physician who'd had any part in her care. Finally, when they had all of that recorded, they did the same with Rhonda's records. There were two physicians who overlapped in both ladies' care. Dr. Juan Perez and Dr. John Garrett had been treating physicians at the hospital during the time and treated them both. Dr. Garrett was the physician that Ahmed had told them about; he had been there the night Rhonda became sick and had continued to treat her. They decided to investigate this lead and call it a night.

They decided on dinner in the hotel restaurant and to get to bed early, hoping to head home first thing in the morning. They had enough information to get a great start and had copied over fifty thousand files to review. Excitement surged inside both of them when they thought about the small lead they had, but a weight of sadness was upon them. Leaving that city, knowing that Ahmed was alone, broke their hearts. His sister dead, a father who was a recluse, and his mother also gone, ate away at them both. Knowing that with a simple word, they could help him and change his life, ease some of the pain in his heart, was almost torture. Aubrey was the weakest and tried to persuade Kayleigh multiple times to go back and tell him; she tried over and over to convince her that they could control him and not blow their cover. But Kayleigh knew they had to have Rhonda safe and secure because if anyone found out, her life would truly be in grave danger. Knowing she was right, Aubrey finally gave up and quietly submitted to her superior's orders.

They boarded a plane for home early the next morning. Sitting on the plane, looking out the window at the beautiful sky as the sun was coming up, Aubrey felt like she was looking at a painting. The sky was a mix of orange and bright fiery-red as the sun crested and announced the dawn of a new day. She felt her heart speed up, and she had a great feeling that this trip would yield promising results. They would be able to see Ahmed soon and give him the best news of his life. The ladies never once noticed that the same man who had followed them from the hospital the previous day had been at the restaurant and was now on the plane with them. He watched them with suspicious, black, small eyes, and they had no idea what was ahead for them.

Kayleigh was trained to be observant and to notice if she was being followed. But this time, she was so involved in looking at the staff directory she did not notice the man. Her eyes danced with excitement when she found the picture of Dr. Garrett. She recognized him, and for the first time, they had a lead in this investigation, finally a tie between the two states and hospitals. The bad thing was, this distraction would be catastrophic for the two women.

CHAPTER 24

Back home, normalcy was a welcomed idea for me. I had missed so much work and had not been as productive as I had in the past. The office decided to hire a physician's assistant named Krissy. She was much younger than me, blond and perky. Since I had been there so long and had the experience, I was expected to train her. Typically, this would have been fine, but I was so distracted with not knowing how Kayleigh and Aubrey were doing that I could barely stand to talk to her. She was engaged to be married and was just starting her new, young career and life. I was envious of her—I couldn't help it; I wanted to start my life over. Take out all the ugly pieces that had made the beautiful puzzle of my life so sad and messed up. I needed to focus and teach her how to make rounds and chart on the patients. Graduating from PA school with honors had made her the top choice for the position, but nothing is like experience, and so much is not even taught in college.

Walking into the hospital during flu season always made me nervous. It was packed with sick patients of all ages. Most of my patients were old, but during this season, age didn't matter. Influenza does not discriminate and is a killer of all ages. This year, the season had been particularly bad with the flu shot being less than 10 percent effective. Deaths were reported every morning on the news, and I never knew what a day in the CCU would hold.

I took the wide-eyed, young PA to the basement level first. This is where the critical care unit held the sickest patients. Some already on life support, some getting ready to be placed on, and others on the way to death. Her long, pale fingers shook when she pushed the elevator button. I smiled to myself, reminiscing when I'd felt that way. I tried so hard to remain positive and enthusiastic to teach her, but in the back of my mind was my daughter and friend out on an ill-fated mission.

The smell of fresh feces greeted us like a foul tropical breeze. The large metal doors opened, and then the wave of air hit us. When there is a fresh bed of diarrhea close by, like I said, a fecal breeze. This odor is often mixed with the aroma of death. A human body is meant to be upright and mobile, but when you are terminally ill and lying in bed, often dependent on machines, your flesh breaks down. I have seen a person's entire buttock literally rot off and fall into the bed. As the pink hue of Krissy's cheeks turned to a mix of green and white, I tried to explain how often people did not have a living will and their families refused to take them off life support. It was actually quite cruel, in my opinion. They could be brain-dead, and the family would not let go. I have never understood how they could see their loved one just lie in the bed, completely sustained by machines. I can honestly say I love my family way too much to do that because I know I will see them again in Heaven. There is a lot we can do in medicine to keep a person alive, but that doesn't mean it is merciful. Sometimes you must love someone enough to let them go. I could tell by the look on the face of the young novice that she was quite overwhelmed. I was not sure if it was me or the smell, to be honest.

The morning was spent going over policies, procedures, and introducing her to various physicians and nurses. She remained nervous throughout the day, and I found myself feeling sorry for her. Her sweet personality and loving heart would make her amazing in this field. She was more intelligent than most of the extenders I had trained in the past, so I was feeling good about her by the end of the day, and I looked forward to helping mold her young mind.

By the time I got home, Tripp had made his famous chicken fajitas, and it was great as always. The dinner conversation was normal, and after casual talk of our day's activities, I quickly helped with the dishes, anxious to get the update from Kayleigh.

I laughed when she told me about the JACHO cover, reminiscing about those days. I was excited to hear more details and help go through the records when they arrived back in town. Knowing she was exhausted, I let her off the phone without drilling her for too much information. Quickly, I shot a text to Aubrey and decided to call it a night.

The house was not quite back in order from our trip, but it always takes so long to get life back on track after a vacation. Tripp had purchased my early Valentine's Day gift, and it sat wrapped in brown packing paper and bubble wrap on the floor of our bedroom. I made a mental note to have Tripp hang it this weekend. Kandinsky was one of my favorite artists, and I had always wanted an original, but of course, financially, that was impossible. This knock-off "Beach in Holland" from his post-impressionism era was gorgeous and one of the highlights of our trip. The $750 he had paid was mere pennies to what the original would have been, but I loved it and could not wait to admire it on my wall daily. I am not sure where my admiration of art had grown from, as I am from a family that had no interest in art and would have found it a waste of money to purchase a piece of artwork that was more than $39.99 at Big Lots.

I wrapped my body up in the soft down comforter and realized I was much more fatigued than I had expected. I would have to adjust to those rigorous days at the hospital. Drifting off to sleep, I let my mind wander back to our trip and the beautiful things we got to see. When we were leaving for the trip to paradise, all was well in my world, but quickly it had come crashing back down the moment I'd met Rhonda. I pushed that back out of my mind and tried to remember good things. The New Year's Eve party that was so fabulous to bring in the New Year, the wonderful dresses, drinks, laughter, and the funny but awkward moment in the library.

Then, suddenly, I sat straight up in the bed. Sweat started to bead up on my forehead, and I had a string of perspiration trickling between my breasts. This seemed to happen repeatedly when I panicked. Despite that, I was shaking so hard the huge sleigh bed began to tremor as if a small earthquake had hit. At that moment, I knew who and what was behind this horrible ordeal, and I also knew what part my husband of twenty-one years played in this true-life horror show.

CHAPTER 25

I knew I had to talk to Kayleigh and barely slept the rest of that night. Once again, I had to put on a fake smile and a white lab coat and go make rounds. That phony smile and cheerfulness had become as much of my work uniform as my stethoscope. The blond beauty was waiting for me with big, anxious eyes when I arrived at the hospital. She had already printed the list of the patients we needed to see and had started taking notes. She was motivated—I had to give her credit. The morning was uneventful, and we once again started in the CCU. I saw Dr. Ricardo, and he enquired about Kayleigh and how she was. I didn't know if it was him or me, but something was odd about the conversation. I decided it was my lack of sleep along with paranoia and continued on. Around one o'clock, I decided we would go to lunch in the doctor's lounge. Taking this time to find out more about Krissy, I was hoping to take my mind off the other dark monsters that were lurking in my subconscious, the ones that were trying to get out and torture me.

She'd been raised in Mooresville, North Carolina, but went to physician's assistant school in Philadelphia. I could not help but get a chill up my spine when she informed me of this. I tried to keep staring down at the pungent fish on my plate and not reveal any of the smoldering emotions inside of me. Finally, when she had stopped talking, I looked up at her. My eyes met the light-blue orbits of this young lady, and we just gazed at each other. The episode was long; I don't think I noticed at first the tears that were tiny, like minute diamonds slowly trickling down her perfect porcelain cheeks. My mind was going in so many different directions. Why was she emotional? Was it that she was homesick, nervous about this new job, fighting with her fiancé? I had learned long ago that young women of this generation seemed to have thin skin and got emotional easier than past generations. But finally, I realized it was none of those things. There was something about the way she looked at me. The gaze was peering into my soul. She wasn't here because this was "such a great job"—she was here because of who I was. The story of what had happened to me had been national news many months ago, but people still remembered and knew what had happened. For some reason, she had sought me out and went to great lengths to work alongside me. I was patient during the long stretch of silence, and finally, after swallowing back tears, she seemed to want to explain. I knew this was not the place to discuss anything private. The doctor's lounge was a constant revolving door of physicians in and out for the free food. I was often amazed that a physician who made close to a million dollars per year made sure they came to eat the disgusting food that was served here daily.

I quickly quieted her and explained we needed to go somewhere private to speak. Unlike the cheap physicians, I didn't care about paying for my meals. We left and went to the local Thai restaurant for lunch. We were quiet on the drive there and waited until we had ordered to start the conversation. It was evident how nervous she was, and once again, she was shaking and having a difficult time hiding her severe anxiety. She started her story by telling me about her best friend, a childhood friend who had gone to PA school with her. They had attended middle school together and were practically sisters. No one knew each other better, and their bond was closer than most blood kin.

Between her words, she would take a drink of her tea, wipe a tear at times. I could tell this was very hard for her; each word seemed to take so much effort for her to get out. My heart was hurting for her, and she had barely gotten started on her story. They had gone to PA school together and lived together; both landed their first real internships at a hospital in Philly. The hairs on my arms started to stand up, and I had that familiar chill start to snake its way down my spine. When she was talking, she took out her phone and pulled up a picture of the young women. She was shorter than Krissy and had black hair cut in a short bob that stylishly framed her perfectly round face. I felt like her big dark eyes were staring straight through me. She looked like a modern version of Snow White.

She was stunning, and her smile looked as if it would be one that would light up even the darkest mood.

As I held her phone in my hand, she talked about the internship and how excited they were to get started in their new career. Her name was Whitley, and she had been a star pupil at the university and had landed the best internship they had. She was working on the cardiothoracic service and loved it. Every night, the ladies would go home and discuss their days—talk about what they had learned and procedures they got to do. Whitley was eager to find a man. School had been rigorous, and she had not had time to date, but now she wanted to make the time. She quickly fell for a young doctor and was swept off her feet, and the time she and Krissy spent together got less and less. Krissy explained she tried not to be jealous but did miss her friend. Then one night, Whitley never came home. Krissy had called and texted and got no response. She had assumed that she was with her new man, but when the next day came and went, she got worried. This was not like her, and she would have never gone this long without checking in.

When the waitress came by and delivered the hot plates of pad thai, I noticed that my previously ravenous appetite had been replaced by nausea. I had the sick feeling I knew where this was going.

Later in the afternoon, Krissy continued to look for Whitley, but it was that night at the hospital she heard the horrible news. Whitley had become very ill while out for dinner and was taken to the ER by Dr. Garrett, the physician she had been seeing. They would not give Krissy a lot of information, and she was forced to wait until her family had arrived to hear the details. Once in the ER, Whitley was thought to have a severe case of cholecystitis, an infected gallbladder. She was taken to the OR for emergency surgery and died intraoperatively.

Knowing that Krissy had sought me out to help her, I tried to stay composed. But my old companion of panic started creeping into the picture. I felt the perspiration start on my forehead and run down my back. The ice in my drink was hitting the side of the glass, and the tremors in my hands increased. She noticed and paused to give me a moment to digest what she had said. She really could have stopped here because I already knew how this story ended.

Proceeding on, she explained how devastated she had been but almost as bad was her confusion. Cholecystitis can start suddenly, but Whitley would have had plenty of time to contact Krissy, and she would have called her—she was certain of that. When she finally saw the physician Whitley had been dating face to face, questioning him had not gone as expected. He had a sarcastic answer for everything, but a huge red flag was his arrogance. She had explicitly asked why Whitley had not called her, and he responded with, "I was with her and was taking care of her. She didn't need to call you." This was when Krissy stated she knew something was not kosher with the story. However, life moved on. She was empty inside and just went through the motions of finishing school. She was lost without her "sister" at her side.

Then she saw the story of my ordeal on the news, and this started a fire within her. She researched it day and night and was able to find details that had not been on the news. This was when she concocted the plan to try to talk to me, but she had known just talking to me would not be enough—she needed to get close to me, to know me. I needed to get to know her and be willing to help her. Getting the job was the only way she could do that. Patiently, she had waited until I was back from traveling and time off to get to work by my side daily. Her original idea was to not bring the topic up until she knew me better, but she was about to burst on the inside to talk to someone about her suspicions. She had tried to reason with Whitley's family about her concerns, but they would not hear of it and kept going back to the fact they had seen her body, seen her buried, etc.

The FBI had kept many details out of the news when it came to my case. The fear of what the public perception would be and the fact that there were more auctions kept the story contained and minimized. But somehow, Krissy had gotten more information than I would have thought possible. The once-tearful blue eyes that were full of sadness had changed to fearless, bright orbs of determination. She was determined that her friend had succumbed to a similar fate, and she would prove it and find her.

I soon realized I sat there with my mouth gaping open with a cold spring roll in my hand. I knew this was a far reach, but it was very possible this was true. The hospital was in Philly, and the physician's name sounded familiar to me. I was not sure where I had heard it, but I recognized it. Mentally, my brain was firing at 1,000 percent. Flashes of my coffin, of Sara, and of Rhonda played like an old silent movie in my mind. I desperately wanted to tell her that her friend had a surgical complication and she was delusional, holding on to a hope that wasn't there, but I could not. I didn't know this for sure and hated to admit she could have been a victim. She was the perfect age, perfectly healthy, and gorgeous. She would have bought a great price at an auction, and I knew this sick fact all too well.

CHAPTER 26

Not being able to talk to Kayleigh and Aubrey that afternoon disturbed me. I knew their flight had landed, and at the very least, Aubrey would have texted me. On my drive home, I tried over and over to reach one of them, but with no response. I could feel a strong sense of something having gone wrong. The connection between a mother and a daughter had been described as supernatural in some instances. My daughter and I are incredibly close, and I felt it—I knew it deep in my soul. Something was wrong. I had no proof, and I spoke aloud to myself in the car to calm down.

My mind was going in so many different directions. I knew the first place Kayleigh and Aubrey would go would be to share the pictures and names with me. But I did not hear a word from either of them. I wasn't sure if the uneasy feeling in the pit of my stomach was due to worry over them or the situation Krissy had just laid in my lap. I knew I had to help her find the truth about Whitley. She had to have closure, and I of all people knew what that feeling was.

I tried to hold myself together to make it home and talk to Tripp. The gulf had continued to widen between us, but when it came to our daughter, I knew he loved no one on this earth more than Aubrey. I had no idea how I would tell him as little as possible about what had been going on and express my concern for our baby girl. Arriving home, I was shocked that he was not there yet. Typically, he arrived at least an hour or two before me. My anxiety continued to climb as I hit redial over and over, trying to locate either of the women who had not been answering me. When I finally went inside, I could immediately tell that Tripp had not been there all day and assumed he had a meeting or something that was making him late, but that odd sixth sense of mine made my mind wonder why he was not here this particular day. As minutes turned to hours, I was scared out of my mind. I can handle a lot of things, but not something happening to Aubrey—not my baby. Finally, Tripp arrived home, and my welcome was anything but warm. As tears streamed down my face, he was greeted with screams of anxiety and panic. He explained he had been at a coaching meeting, and he had told me he would be late, but I must have forgotten. He felt like I was worrying for no reason and Aubrey was old enough to take care of herself. Him trying to *handle* me just infuriated me more.

Trying to sleep that night was pretty much impossible. I paced the floor and continued to burn up their phones. Finally, at about 3:00 a.m. with no luck, knowing that Aubrey's plane had landed over twenty-four hours before, I decided to call someone I knew could help—my favorite FBI agent. I had not spoken to the detective in months, but his number was embedded in my mind. He answered on the first ring, and I knew by his tone of voice he was awake. I did not give him the opportunity to say much, and there were no kind greetings exchanged; I got straight to the point of my call. He already was ahead of me and was searching for the missing agents. You would think I would be relieved, but quite the opposite. I was hoping he would tell me I was being stupid, no reason to worry, but the FBI had not had the check-in that was required when returning from an assignment. Kayleigh was a seasoned agent and was aware of the protocol, which she typically followed by the letter. When I heard his voice, I knew my worst nightmare was coming true. My daughter was missing, along with my best friend. All of the horrible things I had survived during the past year were nothing compared to the utter terror I felt at that moment. I knew I could be a strong woman—a survivor—and I had proven that. But one thing I knew with 100 percent certainty was that I could not survive losing my daughter. I froze in terror while the agent spoke on the phone. I did not hear a lot of what he was saying. I was frozen in that horrible moment, imagining horrific things that may be happening, not even knowing where to start or what to do next.

Finally, when I was able to pull my mind out of the fog it was in. I immediately wanted to meet and start looking. This idea was not met with enthusiasm, but he knew me and knew I was determined and would not just sit at home doing nothing. I got dressed and went to wake up Tripp. I explained more calmly at this hour in the morning where I was going and that Aubrey was, indeed, missing. He was up and awake before I could stop him. He glared at me for not awakening him sooner. Reminding him of his flippant attitude earlier made him recoil his harsh tone. We rode in silence to the FBI's temporary headquarters. I knew there was so much Tripp did not know about, and my mind wondered how to go about this without utterly destroying my marriage once and for all, especially if he was innocent. As luck would have it, the agent knew and quickly had Tripp taken to a briefing room, and he and I could talk in private. He threw question after question at me, wanting to know what either lady had told me about the investigation and what they had found out on the trip. I did not know any more than he did, and we were at a loss. As we awaited the surveillance videos to come in from the hotel and the airport, my anxiety levels were at an all-time high. I knew I needed to pull myself together, so I excused myself and went to the ladies' room. As I looked at myself in the mirror, I was shocked at what I saw.

The person looking back at me was not a person I recognized. The face before me was pale, stressed, and worn. The signs of stress and aging had really begun to make their mark. I was shocked by my appearance. I had always taken pride in how I looked, and I never left the house without making sure my hair was fixed and makeup applied. I was never the kind of person who went out wearing jogging pants and a t-shirt. The lack of sleep and the stress of the last few months had taken a toll on me. I had aged twenty years overnight.

Never being the most attractive woman, I had often wondered the last few months why they even picked me to auction. My appearance had not even crossed my mind in the past twenty-four hours, and I did not have the time or the energy to worry about it then. I washed my face, pulled myself together, and put my hair up in a ponytail.

CHAPTER 27

knew something had happened when I walked out and multiple FBI agents were swarmed around a small screen. You could tell this was not the environment they were accustomed to. The scene reminded me of a piece of candy on the playground on a hot summer day. Bees and ants will swarm around it—these FBI agents resembled that picture. They were tightly gathered around this tiny monitor, trying to push one another aside and see. All were trying to get the proverbial lick of the candy. I, however, was the "Queen Bee," and I pushed my way through. That was my daughter, and I had to know what was going on.

The first video we looked at was from the restaurant. My heart sank, the pit of my stomach ached, and nausea came in waves. My beautiful daughter and my friend were sitting at the table having dinner. You could tell they were tired; I could see the stress on Aubrey's face. I had forgotten how long her hair was. She had turned into such a beautiful young woman. I felt like I had not seen her in years. Tears welled up in my eyes and started to fall. How could I ever survive if something happened to her? But I wasn't watching this video to look at my daughter. We were watching to see what had happened. I shook myself back in focus and concentrated on the surroundings.

We scanned the tables around them, looking for someone alone, someone watching them. We could see from the angle of the security footage who was at the bar. There was nothing really out of the ordinary—your typical creepy people who go to bars were there. Those who sit and drink and wait for the next woman to hook up with. There were half-naked women who looked like they had been battle-worn and were awaiting the next male victim to seduce. Then I noticed, in a dark corner, toward the back, near the kitchen, there was a man. He was nursing a drink, pretending to look at a magazine, trying to be incognito. Every so often, his eyes would shift upward, clearly watching the two women. Chills went through my body almost uncontrollably.

The next video clip was from the airport, with clips from multiple views of the airport terminal. We watched for what seemed like hours as the women went from security to the boarding area. I was exhausted, my lower back aching, and I felt like this was useless. I had no idea when I had eaten last and when I would be able to take a break. But right at that moment, in the boarding line, we saw him. He was intentionally following them, and we could see him peering around the crowd to see them. Anxiety welled up in me when I noticed he had no bags. Obviously, he looked extremely suspicious.

Quickly, the agents were barking orders, doing face recognition, trying to find that hideous stalker.

Then, for some reason, there was fog in the room. I could see it from the corners of my eyes. Tears start to run down my face, and I started to feel dizzy.

I pictured a palm tree in a hurricane, each one so strong. Wind could blow with a dominant force, but they would not break. They just bent and rebounded each time the wind assaulted them. The tall, straight trees were so pliable. They always amazed me, how they didn't break from all of the stress of the relentless winds. That was me—I was like a palm tree; I had been beaten by the wind over and over this past year, almost to a breaking point, but I had rebounded each time. But not today. Seeing the man stalking them follow them on the plane was the end for me. I could not withstand any more force on my body, so I finally broke. That was my baby, and I had no idea how to help her. As I hit the floor, I pictured the tall, strong palm tree, finally ripping apart in the middle. That was me. I was ripped apart.

CHAPTER 28

I didn't remember much after that. Tripp, of course, was distraught. He had an update by the FBI as I was taken to a nearby ER for some fluids. I was dehydrated; my body was exhausted. My husband was by my side, comforting and consoling, trying to be there for me. But as soon as I was awake, my instincts kicked in, and all I could think about was getting my baby girl back. Tripp quickly updated me, telling me that agents were doing all they could to find out who this man was.

Another twelve hours had passed, and no one had heard anything. Powerless, I knew I could not get out of that bed and they were not going to let me leave. Why was I so weak? Why had I let myself pass out? My baby needed me! I was feeling stronger, and the fluids had given me a new sense of renewal. When I was finally able to eat and not have nausea mediation, I could be discharged. Once again in this horrible nightmare, I needed to pick myself up, dust myself off, and find a way to fix this. It was my fault that my daughter had been brought into this, and I was going to make sure she survived.

Finally, after a few hours, I could leave. I agreed to go home, and rest and a hot bath was calling my name. Tripp was trying to take care of me, and I played along. Yes, it's true, I would like for a moment for someone to take care of me. I felt like all I had ever done was take care of other people. Let me assure you, this was only for a moment. I'll admit I was weak, but I was pulling my stuff together, I knew I had to.

I poured myself some Diet Mountain Dew, submerged myself in a hot bubble bath, and laid back. There would be no way under God's green earth I could sit idly by and rely solely on the FBI when they had been pathetic this entire investigation. I wasn't going to be one of those moms that sit there, cry, and wait to hear that my daughter was found dead. I looked comfortable and relaxed when Tripp came to check on me. But make no mistake, my mind was formulating a plan on how to find out who had Aubrey.

Whoever had followed them had most likely started following them at the hospital. I wasn't sure, but we all knew it had something to do with the ladies going and asking too many questions. They had found something they should not have. The trip had started at Ahmed's apartment, I needed to get there and talk to him. I needed to retrace their steps. How was I going to do this? Knowing they probably would never let me leave, I decided I would have to be upfront with the agent. Heck, I had done it before, and it had worked out. After I had soaked away the hellish events of the previous forty-eight hours, I got out, dried off, and put on fresh clothes and fresh makeup. Then I put on an "armor of courage," so to speak. Come heck or high water, I would find my daughter and my friend. And after all this was over, I would make sure the people who were responsible for this, who had ruined my life, would pay. As I dried my hair and after my makeup was applied, I had a revelation: I had a job!

Like a ton of bricks, I remembered I had a job. I didn't know how I still had a job, but I did. So once again, I called to let them know I would not be in, and then it hit me. Krissy! I had completely forgotten that she had exposed herself to me. I had been so wrapped up in my current situation that I'd forgotten about hers. While I continued to get ready, my mind went back to the story she had told me. Immediately, excitement started to surge through me. Krissy was from that area; Krissy had worked at that hospital, and she may recognize that man! I didn't know how I could do it, but I needed to get the FBI to let Krissy help us.

The FBI hates to involve civilians, but she could possibly recognize him. It would mean a major break in the case and help find my daughter. I called the agent; I had already told him the story that Krissy had relayed to me, but our focus for the last few hours was to find the two missing agents. Of course, he was hesitant. But what would it hurt to let her look at the footage? Once I finally got him to agree, I called Krissy. She was on her way to the hospital to see patients, and I started to quickly explain the events that had happened. She agreed to immediately meet me. I gave her the address of the small, makeshift FBI headquarters, and we agreed to meet shortly. Finally! Finally, a breakthrough. If Krissy could recognize this man, it could mean finding my daughter. I quickly updated Tripp, and of course, he insisted on going with me. Looking back, it amazed me how I completely forgot about Tripp being part of this, because I knew beyond a shadow of a doubt my husband would never hurt his baby girl. The thought of selling me could be possible, but that man loved his daughter. He would never have allowed this to happen.

Krissy beat us to the FBI headquarters. I could see anxiety etched across her beautiful, young face. She was trembling, and I wasn't sure if it was excitement, anxiety, or nervousness about what she was about to see. We sat in a little room outside the viewing area. The agents had the video footage adjusted for better picture and better quality. Large TV screens had taken the place of the small monitor we had all tried to look at the day before. Technology truly amazed me; the faces on the screen was so much better on these TVs. The technicians had done an amazing job of filtering out the video footage. The footage from the restaurant wasn't as good as the airport; you really could not distinguish the facial features as well. But in the airport, the video was much better, for obvious reasons.

Krissy just stood there, arms folded, a solemn look on her face. You could tell she was quite intimidated by the FBI agents around her. She never said anything; I don't even think I saw her blink for the longest time. I stared at her intently, waiting, wanting some semblance of recognition to cross her face. Then finally it happened. When the man handed the airline agent his boarding pass, you could see his face clearly. Immediately, every bit of color drained from Krissy's face. Her lower lip started to tremble and shake; for just one moment, I thought she might pass out. She was terrified at that moment, but I was excited! We had a lead—she recognized this man, and we all knew it immediately. Seeing her reaction, Agent Johnson got her a chair, barked orders at the others to get her a glass of water, and I, of course, went to drill her. We had to let her calm down; we had to let her mind process what she had just seen.

Other agents who weren't assisting in the case were asked to leave the room. The agent started calmly, in a very sweet tone of voice, asking her questions. She had recognized the man. He was a physician's assistant named Dean Kepler. He'd worked for the cardiology group at that same facility. He was handsome, charismatic, and loved by everyone. The thing that had really freaked her out was that the physician who had treated Whitley was best friends with Kepler. Once again, I had to feel sorry for her, but at the same time, the excitement rose inside me, I was so happy at that moment. We had a lead! We had a name! Let's go! Let's go get my baby. I wanted to grab him and find out what they had done with Aubrey. I didn't want to wait another second. I started to pace the floor, but after the look of death from the agent, I sat back down. He patiently asked me to calm down, and I finally was able to contain my excitement. But in my mind, every second we wasted there was another second that my daughter would be missing and her life would be in danger. He immediately put out an APB for Dean Kepler.

Soon, information started coming in about Mr. Kepler. Krissy was able to pull herself together and tell us a little more about him. He was young and good-looking, never had any problems with the ladies. He always liked to drive elaborate vehicles, travel to exotic places, and live very lavishly. I knew what a PA's salary was, and I knew he could not afford all the things he did on that salary. She went on to talk about how he had been such good friends with the physician who had dated Whitley. He was not like the cockier, rude physician who she despised so much. He was always friendly and sociable, and she revealed to us that she could hardly believe that he would have anything to do with this. These were details I simply didn't care about. I just wanted to run out the door and find my daughter. The rational side of me knew this could not happen immediately. After a while, they had to address the details about Mr. Kepler's whereabouts, and the plans were being made to go ahead and start looking for places he could've taken the ladies near the airport.

They had boarded the plane that had landed in Charlotte, North Carolina. The video footage was being requested from the Charlotte Douglas Airport, but for some reason, it was taking more time than expected. While they were waiting, I could not help but think that they may have left Charlotte. Or North Carolina, for that matter. No one really knew the extent of this crime ring. I was doubtful that the headquarters for this nefarious business was in North Carolina; it could be in a completely different state. They could have boarded the plane, or another vehicle could have been waiting to take them anywhere. I was not about to wait around and do nothing. Tripp felt the same way. He was anxious and tired of feeling helpless. He kept trying to get the most amount of information he could, but eventually, I could tell that he was getting irritated and restless.

By this time, Krissy was tired of being drilled. She wanted to do something; she wanted to help me. Ultimately, helping me would also help her find what she needed. Was Whitley still alive? Had she been taken somewhere? Had she been auctioned off? Eventually, she asked to be excused to go to the ladies' room. I decided I would go with her, and we took this opportunity to try to talk. She felt the same way I did. Privately, she explained that she felt confident that our girls would not be in North Carolina. She had done so much more research, digging more thoroughly before talking to me. She felt like many physicians at the medical center had been involved. A lot of her thoughts were speculation. However, she had thoroughly researched the topic and was extremely concerned. We were trying to concoct a plan when a female FBI agent came into the restroom to wash her hands, so our talk was cut short.

We went back out and joined the others to only hear the alarming news. For some odd reason, there were no security cameras or security footage from when the ladies exited the aircraft. There had been a computer glitch, and the footage had all been erased from the entire terminal to the parking decks. I knew this was not a coincidence. This business ran so deep, it was like an evil octopus that had tentacles everywhere from funeral homes to physicians, surgeons' respiratory therapists to businessmen. With so many people involved, who knew—it wouldn't take much to bribe someone at the airport to adjust the cameras. The lead ended there. They were able to find out that Mr. Kepler had not been on his job for the last month. He'd been fired for some false documentation, and no record of employment was found anywhere else. His license to practice was still active, but by looking at the registries, we saw that he had not been prescribing any medications.

I pulled Krissy aside with Tripp, and in the spur of the moment, I had a plan. I was going to Philly, and I was going to find this hospital. I was going to retrace the steps Kayleigh and Aubrey had taken. I was going to locate this man's house and do what I needed to do. Also, it would be of benefit to touch base with Ahmed. I mean, who knew, he may have known the guy, and at this point, anything would help.

CHAPTER 29

Krissy immediately was on board with my plan, but of course, Tripp was not. She felt like it was a great idea to go investigate; she knew the people, and she had a way in. She still even had her ID badge. I decided I would go ahead and let Agent Johnson know about my plan, and surprisingly, he took it quite well. Possibly because he felt like I would be in his way here, but also, at this point, I think he was open to anything that would help. He was quite upset about the loss of his agent. He wanted her back, and he needed her to be safe. It didn't take long to arrange the flight; I was amazed at how quickly the FBI could come up with a fake ID for me. They felt like I was possibly being watched, and the people would be looking for my name and my face. The only way I could go was if I would agree to change my appearance. They could not risk me disappearing and have another missing person to worry about. Of course, they would have FBI follow us from a distance, but there was always a risk.

My hair had always been long and dark. The past few years, the gray had started to show up, slowly, like weeds invading a flower garden. My hair was something that usually looked good. Curly, always styled, and I will admit, it was very pretty—people always commented. So, when the female agent came through and decided I was going to get a new short haircut, I was a little disturbed, to stay the least. But, I reasoned, it was just hair, and I would shave my head if it got my baby home. So, after a new cut, highlights, and colored contacts, I had to admit I looked very different. I had a new identity and name, and we were on the way.

The FBI had arranged a driver to pick us up. The first place I wanted to go was to visit Ahmed. I needed to know if he recognized any of the men or if any had been involved with them. For all we knew, he may be friends or had been with them at some point. Any tiny piece of information would help us. We had no time to call or make arrangements with him; things had moved too fast. It was early morning, and I was hopeful the young man would be home. The excitement surged through me; for some reason, I felt like we would get what we needed soon, and I practically beat the door down.

I was like a deflated balloon when after ten minutes of knocking, no one came to the door. Tears started to come, and I had to swallow hard to get them in control as we slowly walked away. As we got back into the agent's car, I noticed a dark young man walking toward my window. Instantly, I was nervous. The tall young man, in dark sunglasses, looked very intense and serious. Out of instinct, the agent reached for his gun in defense. The young man came closer and closer to my window and just stood there and stared intently at me. I slowly made a small crack in the window, and all he said was, "I am Ahmed." It took a moment for my slow, fatigued brain to process who was looking at me. He turned and walked quickly away before I could even fully open the window or door. Krissy was getting out of the back as I was jumping out of the front. The agent started to follow, but I stopped him. Ahmed was not heading back to his apartment, but one on the lower level of the building. When we finally caught up, he motioned us to not talk until we had gone into a small door in the back of the building. After I got some semblance of direction, I realized we would be almost directly underneath his apartment. The room we entered was a storage unit. I assumed each apartment had one. There was dim lighting, and on the back of a table, some computers were set up. I could see more when my eyes acclimated to the dim light. He had a camera set up and multiple TV screens, all watching the outside of his apartment door and some monitoring the interior. Realizing he had seen us knocking, I just stood and looked at him. Intense eyes glared back at me, and he asked us to take a seat. He was visibly upset, cautious. I could not help but wonder what had happened to make him so defensive when he didn't know us or why we were even here. Silence hung awkwardly in the room.

"Why are you here?" asked Ahmed. "I know who you are, and I want to know *why are you here?*" His voice trembled with anxiety—or was this anger? As his tone climbed an octave, I was taken back and just stood there for a moment before I spoke. He could see he had startled me, and a flash of regret went across his face.

"I am Layla Matthews, and I need your help." Before I even finished my sentence, he held up his hand and shook his head.

"I said I know who you are; I know your daughter was here and lied to me. I will not answer any questions until I know what is going on. Since the visit with your daughter, I have been followed, and my apartment was broken into. I know the story she told me was a lie. I knew it even before I was followed. Your daughter wanted to reach out to me. Her eyes, they pierced my soul. She stood at my door and stared at me before her and the other lady left. I knew she needed to tell me something but could not." His voice started to tremble as he spoke. His tone was soft now and vulnerable. Tears began to pool in his eyes.

Knowing my daughter as I do, I could about guarantee that my Aubrey was instantly smitten by this handsome, young man. He paused and waited for a response. Politely, he offered us a seat; I had almost forgotten Krissy standing beside me. So, we sat at a table with electronics thrown haphazardly all around. After a brief silence, I started to explain. I knew that they had not shared anything with him on their visit for the safety of Rhonda and him, but I was past that—I needed his help.

He apparently could handle himself, so I started by asking him exactly what he knew, hoping that would save some time. He reluctantly began to repeat what he had revealed about being followed and told us about how he knew someone had been in his apartment multiple times. The strange thing was they never took anything. A person who was not observant would have never known, but he did. So, he placed small cameras and began to monitor his own apartment. He told us how a couple of men would come in and look in his computer, his emails, his searches, look at his mail, then leave. They wanted to know if he was searching for someone or something. They wanted to know what "research" he was doing. Of course, they found nothing. But in his secret area, he had done a lot of work. He had found out who Aubrey was but not Kayleigh. After figuring out about my daughter, he looked into her history, and thanks to social media, he connected the dots and discovered my story. He never admitted what he was thinking, but I had a feeling he already knew.

He stopped abruptly and said, "Now your turn—what is going on? And how does this involve me?"

So, I started my story. He had a vast range of emotion as I gave a very abbreviated synopsis and told him about me and the body auction. He sat on the edge of the chair the entire time, hands folded on his lap, with perfect posture. When I got to the part about the Dominican Republic and started to explain, he suddenly slumped into the chair. His olive complexion was instantly pale. I don't recall ever seeing color leave someone's face so dramatically before. My heart hurt for him. I could feel tears falling from my eyes, and before I knew it had even happened, I was crying as I talked. I did not stop; I kept talking because I was afraid if I paused, I could not start back. Emotions poured as I recounted the nightmare I had lived. I felt Krissy's hand lay on my thigh in comfort. He never interrupted, never asked a question, just listened. I went on to explain why the ladies had come and why they had to deceive him. He nodded his head at this point, which was the first sign that he was still breathing in what seemed like forever.

Finally, when I was done and had told him about Aubrey and Kayleigh not returning home, he sat up on his chair again. He slowly went to a small mini bar in the corner of the room and offered us a drink. My mouth was like the Sahara, so I gladly accepted some water. As he turned around, his face shocked me. He had transformed from a shocked, sad brother to a determined, fierce fighter. Just his expression gave me a renewed sense of hope. The fierce determination in his eyes and across his face made me shudder. He absorbed the information, processed it, and was ready to move. Krissy stood to move from the confined space, and that is when he first seemed to notice she was even there. He enquired about her involvement, and she tried to explain. The first words from her tiny pink lips were scared and timid. But she was able to wrap her story into a fast review and revealed she had a loved one to also be located.

We all had a common bond—we had a loved one who needed to be found. I had a deep, dark feeling that we didn't have a lot of time left.

CHAPTER 30

For the most part, I feel okay with my computer skills—well, I should say I *did* until I met Ahmed. He immediately wanted to know the names and get the pictures of the physicians we were looking into. Seeing how things were going and feeling good that he was not a "loose cannon," so to speak, I called the agent and updated him. When he asked to speak to Ahmed himself, I was shocked but handed Ahmed the phone. After what I assume was a few short pleasantries, he went to the FBI database. After a few strokes, he was in and looking at photos. Some of the faces, Krissy recognized, and others she did not. I stood there in shock and wondered where these profiles had come from. How had the FBI concocted this list so quickly, or had they had it the whole time?

As I saw Dr. Pierce's face appear on the screen, I froze. But what astounded me was that Krissy knew him. We had gone through so many pictures by now, and when either of them noted a familiar face, he would stop, take down the information, and relay to the agent, who was now on speakerphone.

"I remember him!" Krissy said anxiously. I was already in a state of shock seeing the face of a demon, so her shrill voice about made me jump out of my skin.

Simultaneously, the agent and I both said, "You do?"

She nodded and said, "He was a physician at the hospital when I first started my clinical rotation in college. He looked younger then, but that's him. His name was Dr. Foulks when he worked with us. He worked in a large hospital group and did some of the education in the clinical rotation for the PA program. He was always creepy—he gave a lot of us girls a weird feeling, if you know what I mean.

"He always loved to brag on Whitley, telling her how smart and pretty she was. She ate it up, loving the extra attention he gave her. I warned her a few times to stay away from him, but she trusted everyone." Krissy went on to explain that he stopped working there a few years ago and never crossed her mind until now. The agent asked her about his friend group, which other physicians he hung out with, so to speak. She tried to recall and was able to come up with a few names. Ahmed's fingers made quick work of his task at hand. On the other screen, he had already pulled up a nationwide physician directory. I had no idea this database even existed, but he started to type in the names she mentioned. As she spoke, I could hear Agent Johnson in the background giving orders to other agents to do what Ahmed was already doing. She could not remember a lot of names. However, she did better than I would expect. But really, a hospital is like any job—there are cliques and groups that migrate toward one another.

The hospitalist groups were always a tight-knit bunch, and then you had the new, younger physicians. They were always the most obnoxious group and drove everyone insane. They swarmed together like a group of tropical fish. They were bright and fresh, lab coats clean and crisp. They were ready to "heal the world." It was always the same—they thought they were smarter than the ignorant nurses, more up to date than the older physicians, and always the best-looking. The men were usually arrogant and ready to bed any young nurse who will let them, and the females—well, they were trying to prove they could make it in a man's world. This made them a group of barracudas with a chip on their shoulder and something to prove. It typically took about a year before they were knocked off the perches on which they'd placed themselves. They either killed a patient or came close to it, then they realized the best teacher in medicine is experience.

The surgeons also tended to hang together, even though they secretly competed with one another and constantly debated on who was the best at his craft.

The specialty groups like cardiology and pulmonary also had a little clique in which they would band together to get what they wanted. But the constant argument over the patient's cause of shortness of breath could throw a little drama in the mix. Pulmonary would argue it was the heart, but cardio would guarantee it was the lungs. It was an old fight that never ceased.

My favorite group was the older physicians. The ones who walked with a limp because their hips and backs were worn out from years of caring for others. Their lab coats were not fresh and starched; they were yellow with various ink spots and marks of the occasional bodily fluids. They laughed at the new groups that came and swooped in to save the day when they screwed up. Their days of torrid affairs with nurses were long gone, and they knew their careers were coming to an end. They were the old-fashioned physicians who still hugged their patients and told them they loved them because they did. Some have had the same patients for over thirty years and are emotionally attached to them. When they die, it hurts them— they are the true healers in the hospital. I fear as these men and women retire a great part of medicine will die with them. With hospitals being about money and new government regulations, health care is not what it used to be. Patients are numbers, not people.

My mind wandered back to a time when my life was just about medicine. I could hear the background noise of the others talking, pictures popping up, and the low hum of the computers working hard to meet the demand of Ahmed's assault against their tiny keys.

I thought of my old friends, my coworkers who I actually spent more time with than my own family.

I was jolted out of my trance of remembrance by Krissy tugging my arm. She sounded like she was in a tunnel. As I cleared my mind out of the fog it was in, my eyes began to focus on the screen in front of me. I stood there looking like a complete idiot, mouth gaping open and the beautiful face on the screen staring back at me. I had a flashback of the night in my bedroom opening my picture to hang it, and the revelation I had at that moment. Being so engulfed with the situation at hand, I had forgotten what I had discovered that night. As Krissy was yelling and trying to snap me out of my stupor, my body was frozen, but my mind was at record speed, processing what I was looking at and hearing. The attractive face appeared on the screen, and Ahmed said that this physician was one of the men who had taken care of his sister. Everyone froze until Krissy came unglued. I could hear Agent Johnson yelling on the speakerphone for me to respond. At that moment, we knew—we all knew who the leader and mastermind was. The entire time, he was right in front of us. It all made sense now, and we also knew where our girls were!

CHAPTER 31

We all had a different agenda. Agent Johnson and I wanted to find Kayleigh and Aubrey. Ahmed, of course, wanted to jump a plane to Dubai, and Krissy wanted to get answers as to what had happened to Whitley. We knew more physicians were involved, but at that moment, we had what we needed. Immediately, Krissy and I were rushed to the airport. My heart racing and the anticipation of what was going to happened were almost too much to stand. The FBI had already arranged for Tripp to be picked up and taken to the FBI headquarters.

I had messaged Agent Johnson over and over, and he was not responding. I knew what they were doing and where they were going. When the plane landed, a car was waiting on us. We were taken to the headquarters, where Tripp was waiting, along with many other agents. The large screens and speakers were playing step by step what was getting ready to happen.

I could see on the screen in front of me the footage on the body cam of the agent approaching the door. How could

I have been so stupid? I should have known who was behind this from the start. Sometimes you just get blinded by loyalty for someone and don't see the facts in front of you. The evidence had been right in front of us the entire time. I was sick to my stomach.

The agents were going in the front door and into a large foyer—one I recognized well. The same décor as I remembered, and the familiar feeling of betrayal crept inside of me. It did not appear anyone was at home; they went from room to room looking for the ladies. One agent would enter a room, check it, and clear it. This went on for what seemed like forever, and no signs of Aubrey or Kayleigh anywhere! I was about to explode from the inside out. The next room was the most familiar to me. My mind went back to a night that seemed like a lifetime ago.

The average salary for a hospitalist is $230,000. This can vary greatly depending on procedures, time worked, patient population, etc. Physicians tend to have extravagant tastes, and this means some work extra shifts or locum jobs for extra cash.

As I stood there and waited for this nightmare to unfold, my mind wandered back to when the first clues should have resonated like beacons in the dark. A Mark McGwire seventieth-home-run baseball is worth three million dollars; "The Madonna and Child Being Crowned by Two Angels" painting is priced at $240,000. How had I not realized that it would have been almost impossible for Dr. Ricardo to afford such a lavish lifestyle on his salary? I had realized it the night that I unwrapped my imitation painting. I had just put it out of my mind, thinking I was wrong. He was such a great guy, my friend, and a smart physician. Why would he do such a horrible thing to so many innocent people? Was money that important to him?

As the camera swept the library, there were no signs of anything. I wondered if they were even in the house. Had he taken them somewhere else? Then, at a quiet moment, we heard a small sound like a tapping noise. Someone was trying to send a signal. The agents searched and tried to determine where the noise was coming from. Apparently, it was from an area of the library, but where?

Safe rooms have become popular among the wealthy. The fear of an intruder and robbery prompted this fad. The rooms are well hidden and not able to be found unless you know where they are located. Libraries are a perfect spot due to the multiple ways to hide the door and the lever to open it. Finally, after over an hour, the panel was discovered and opened. I had just about lost my mind waiting, so I had driven over to the house. I had to see Aubrey, touch her and hold her. I made it just as the door opened. There had been no signs of the maniac who owned the home yet. There had been an APB placed for him already, so I figured he was out of the country by now. The large metal door, concealed by a large bookshelf, opened, and I sobbed as I saw my daughter walk out. We embraced and cried for the longest time. The smell of her skin, the feel of her tiny frame in my arms was the best thing I had ever felt next to the day I held her in my arms for the first time. I wasn't even aware that Kayleigh had not come out. When my mind cleared, I pulled Aubrey back to get a look at her and realized the look of devastation on her face. Kayleigh wasn't with her; he had taken her in the middle of the night and left. Neither had been hurt—they had just been locked away in the safe room—but then Kayleigh had been taken. Aubrey explained to us how he had intended to take her instead, but Kayleigh put up such a fight, she was taken. Once again, I owed Kayleigh my life.

The whole house was blocked off, and dozens of FBI and CIA agents flooded the property. Computers were loaded, and the entire home was picked over from top to bottom. A dark van pulled up, and Tripp came running to greet his baby; then another man—Ahmed—came up behind him. I was quite surprised to see him. He had gotten a flight after we left to come and assist the FBI in getting his sister home. His determination was so intense, his face stern and serious. When Aubrey was finally out of the bear hug her father held her in, she turned to Ahmed. Typical Aubrey reached up to adjust her hair in the presence of a hot male. She walked slowly and almost awkwardly over to where he stood. He was a good six feet tall, and she looked so small at five feet three inches. She gazed up at him, and tears started once again to flow. She tried to say how sorry she was that she had to lie to him, but before she could finish, he took a finger and placed it over her trembling lips. He nodded and told her he understood. Then in an odd gesture, he reached down with his big, muscular arms and embraced my tiny daughter. He hugged her long and tight. At first, I was shocked, but I guess anyone would have had to be blind not to see the instant chemistry that radiated from them.

Even in this horrible situation, there seemed to be a spark of electricity in the air.

We decided to go back to our house and wait for other information to come in. Aubrey needed to shower and clean up, and I was also exhausted and needed to refresh. Ahmed politely informed me that he would be in touch and he would let me know what hotel he would be staying at. I instantly informed him he would not be at a hotel and invited him home with us. Awkwardly, he accepted, and I think I saw him blush a little. We were loaded up in an FBI van and taken home. I don't think I took my tight grip off of Aubrey the entire time.

CHAPTER 32

arkness, coldness, a hard table on her bare back. Kayleigh tried to clear her mind; what had happened? Where was she? She remembered the tiny pinch of pain that had hit her in the arm right before total darkness shrouded around her. She had been given an injection; she was sedated. Now she had no idea how long she had been out or where she had been taken. She tried to stay calm, get her thoughts together, and assess the situation. Panic would only be another enemy right now, and if she wanted to survive, she did not need another foe. She could tell by the way her body felt, her sore and stiff joints, that she had not moved her extremities in hours. She must have been given a potent medication. When she tried to take a deep breath, the bottom of her lungs ached and burned. She had been shallow breathing for a few hours.

She could hear no outside noises around her. Just darkness and total silence. When she tried to lift her head, she could not, and her arms were restrained beside her. Her heart rate started to speed up, as she could not help but to feel a sense of doom. Kayleigh realized this may be the time she did not survive. She replayed the events in her mind, still mad at herself for not knowing what was happening around her.

The past few months had been some of the happiest in her life. She had not really had the luxury of dating or being involved with a man, but with this ongoing case, she was able to relocate near her new friends. She had grown to love Aubrey and my family. Then the extra benefit of Dr. Ricardo had made it a perfect storm. They had been attracted to each other from the beginning. It never occurred to her throughout this time that he could have been involved. As she thought back and remembered the photo album and the trips, she remembered that he was in those. Had she suspected then? Why hadn't she? It should have been obvious that he was involved, but by then, her heart was affected, and like it so oftentimes did, it outweighed what her brain was telling her. They had taken romantic trips; he had given her fabulous gifts and expressed that he had fallen in love with her. She felt the sting of her hot tears falling down her face onto the cold table. She had also fallen in love with this man, but how could she not? He was so handsome, sweet, and charming. The perfect man for any woman. She had opened herself up to finally trust and fall in love, and he was a psychopath!

After the New Year's Eve party, things had really started to heat up for them. The holiday season always brings out the best in people, and romance is often sparked. Everyone in the beautiful dresses and tuxedos, the champagne and gifts. It was a fairytale for her. That night, when all the guests had left, he told her he was falling in love with her. She had not told anyone, but they had spent the night together for the first time and became intimate. She had not been with a man in many years; the nervousness and anxiety made it even more special. They had enjoyed each other's bodies and not slept the entire night. They were together many, many times after that, and each time seemed to be more intense. But this had all been a lie! He had known the whole time she was FBI and hid it. She had almost revealed to him one night who and what she actually was but decided not to, as she was worried about his safety. How ironic!

When she and Aubrey had landed at the airport that day, she had already discovered something was wrong. On the plane, she had gone to the lavatory and noticed a man that she had seen at the hotel and restaurant the day before. She knew they had been followed, and she had missed it. But they could not do anything while on the plane, so she went back to her seat and informed Aubrey of her concern. When they landed, they quickly had each other's back and exited the plane first. Aubrey had spoken to the attendant and flashed her FBI credentials, and they were allowed off the plane before anyone else. They headed out to the ground transport when they had seen a familiar face. Her knight in shining armor, Dr. Ricardo, was loading his Porsche SUV with his suitcase when they saw him. He explained that he was just returning from a seminar. Of course, he offered them a ride, and, needing to get out of the airport quickly, they accepted. He had offered them to have a quick refreshment at his house before they went on home, and the ladies had agreed. It was evident to her now that the drugs were in the drinks, and they did not wake up in the safe room for hours. Kayleigh had never been so shocked. She was angry and heartbroken all at the same time. Aubrey had comforted her and reassured her that no one knew, and he was excellent and brilliant at his part in this. When he had come in to see them, he looked at Kayleigh for a long time. It seemed he had feelings for her; his eyes looked sad and regretful. He tried to talk to her, but after only one word, she had spit in his face.

The ladies had no idea what had happened that made him come into the safe room the day she was taken. He was anxious, yelling at someone on the phone, and had decided he had to leave and make a clean break. He had grabbed Aubrey, but Kayleigh could not let him take her. She was so young and had her whole life ahead of her. She had fought and got a few good hits in, and it appeared he was in such a rush, he just gave up and settled for Kayleigh. By the few things she heard on the phone call before she passed out, she was a "payment." He was being taken somewhere and protected, but there was a price. And of course, it would be a woman.

This was when it all came back to her: yes, she was the payment for his safety. He was relocating due to the "heat" being too much in the United States, but whomever he was on the phone with needed a payment. He had told them how young and beautiful Aubrey was, but when Kayleigh had gone so crazy on him, he'd settled for her instead. He was in too big of a rush to fight any longer. One of the other men was to come by the house later and "take care of Aubrey."

Kayleigh felt herself start to panic. Aubrey. She was left locked in the safe room. She had seen many safe rooms, and his was a very state-of-the-art one. She knew that no one suspected Dr. Ricardo; they probably would not look for them at his house. No one would know Aubrey was there, and she would either be killed by someone or starve in the hidden room. But something had to have happened for him to panic, someone had to have figured something out, or he would not have had to run. Kayleigh continued to try to calm herself. As the time passed, she became more and more lucid. Her muscles ached, and she was so thirsty.

She replayed the events of the past year over and over in her mind. Working with the FBI had been something she would have never dreamed of doing, but it had been the most amazing experience of her life. She had made lasting friendships and loved the people she worked with. She had grown to call them her family.

Then, suddenly, a painful stimulus shot into her brain. It was a blinding light, and when it had been turned on, it felt like a gun to her head. Her eyes were on fire, and it took a few moments to be able to focus. Finally, when she could see who had entered the room, she was shocked. These men were not American; they did not speak English. They were not dressed in clothes that she recognized at all. She tried to talk to them, as she knew a few languages, but they were speaking a slang form of Arabic, and she could not understand anything they were saying. They kept talking, ignoring her repeated pleas for release. She was dirty, hungry, and cold. She looked around her and saw she was in a type of basement. She had been restrained to a large metal table in what appeared to be a small makeshift examining room. Fear gripped her, as she felt like she remembered this scene like in a movie she had seen before. This looked a lot like the room where the men had prepared the women for the auction. Not as elaborate, but similar. The men looked at her, touched her hair, and started to examine her, still ignoring her screaming at them. When one of them tried to open her mouth and look at her teeth, she bit him. He slapped her across the face so hard her ears rang loudly for a few minutes. One of the men grabbed a syringe from a table close by and gave her an injection. The instant warmth went through her veins. She was awake but calm and subdued. This was not the potent medication she had been given to get here because she was still awake and aware of what was going on. The men proceeded to examine her. One examined her breasts and the other her genitals. She could tell they had to be physicians and they knew what they were looking for. She was self-conscious because she knew she had not bathed in days and had urinated on herself multiple times since she had not had any other option.

The men yelled out of the door, and some women came in. They left the room, and she was given a bath, right there in that cold room. They carried basins of warm water in and baskets of oils and all types of creams. She was in and out of sleep but would wake up when her hair was rinsed or the occasional wild hair plucked by tweezers. She knew in her rational mind, when it was able to break through, what was happening. She knew what this prep meant. They were disposing of her by selling her, trading her. There was nothing she could do about it—absolutely nothing.

CHAPTER 33

It's amazing what a hot shower can do. It can wake you up, refresh you, and wash away dirt and sadness. One by one, Aubrey, Ahmed, and I emerged refreshed and renewed. We all had a new "fight" in our veins. I was ready to find that demon, rescue my friend, and help Ahmed get to Rhonda. He would have the records we needed and know how to get them both. Krissy had been exhausted and went home to get some rest also. There had been an elaborate computer system located in the safe room. The web addresses of multiple sites on the dark web revealed the way the men advertised the auctions. There were lists of hospitals all over the world that had contacts and physicians who were participants of the human auction. The amount of information they were able to recover was astounding. Agent Johnson was shocked that it had been left behind, but most likely, Dr. Ricardo did not think the room would ever be found—or when it was, it would be so far into the future that it would be too late. Also, these computers could be erased from a remote area, so the agents worked around the clock to get what they could from them. This was all encouraging, but one thing that was upsetting was that we all realized the physicians we knew had disappeared could be at any of these hospitals around the world being sheltered by their counterparts.

Ahmed went to work quickly on trying to decide the best route to get to his sister. He was rational and knew this had to be handled correctly or the consequences could be devastating. This was a different country, and the man who had purchased his sister was rich and powerful. There could be diplomatic ramifications as well as harm to Rhonda. He was an Egyptian but had been born and raised in the USA. He only spoke very little Arabic and did not have the contacts needed to help him in that country, but he knew someone who did. He had informed me that he had a guest coming, and when the doorbell rang, I was in shock at who I welcomed.

At my door stood a tall, dark man. His face was weary and worn. Lines of stress and worry crossed it, and his demeanor was harsh and cold. Ahmed quickly introduced him as his father, Ishmael. He had called him and spoken to him while he was on the way here. Trying not to go into great details over the phone, he explained that Rhonda could be alive, so of course, he came immediately. Once again, we had to replay the events that had happened over the past year. Each time was like a knife to my chest, and I felt like it took more out of me every time I had to repeat the details. He sat there and listened in utter shock.

He had been a physician. From what Ahmed briefly explained, he was actually a world-renowned physician with an extensive medical practice. The thing that made him so extraordinary was his memory. He never forgot anything. A date, a diagnosis, a name. He was absolutely brilliant. People looked up to him and respected him more than any physician he had ever known. He had changed when his wife had died; he could not handle being able to save other people but not the love of his life. But when Rhonda died also, well, that was all it took to make him retire and move to Florida. He lived as a recluse, shutting himself off from everyone and everything.

Many emotions crossed his face, but the main one was intense and violent anger. When I started to talk about Rhonda, his fist was so tightly clenched that his olive knuckles looked white as chalk. At one point, he hit my glass table so hard I was certain either his hand was broken or the table.

He seemed so appalled by this business and these physicians, he had a tough time comprehending it. He asked the same questions over and over, and I continued until he was up to date on what we all knew. He immediately knew why Ahmed had asked him to come. He had family in Dubai, he knew people there, and he'd been raised in Cairo. His Arabic was flawless, so we had a way in!

When Agent Johnson arrived, we knew something was wrong, but I had a feeling nothing at this point could stop this man from getting to his daughter. He did not care about diplomacy or danger; he was getting his daughter, and he was getting her soon!

CHAPTER 34

Rhonda looked at her surroundings; the room was elaborate, almost obnoxiously so. The enormous bed and everything was gold; she could not help but laugh at the ostentatious lifestyle of her capturer. She was able to walk around more freely now that her husband felt he could trust her. It was more like he felt as if he had trained her to be submissive. In the beginning, she had tried to escape and tried to talk the staff into helping her. She was beaten many times, always in a way that no scars where left, her perfect skin never marked. There were times when she would be locked in the dark for days at a time as punishment. Finally, she realized there had to be another way. She would have to "play along" with this narcissistic maniac if she were to have a chance of escape. All hope had been lost until she had met me on vacation. Her passion and the fact that she knew what had happened to her gave her new hope. She dreamed daily of being rescued from the hell she was in.

She was Egyptian by heritage but had been born in the United States. She had only known equality for women and free speech, and even though women are not entirely equal to men in some aspects such as salaries, they were not "slaves" of men in the US. She had never had to submit to every wish of a man. Only speaking when allowed and having to obey. She knew that other countries still treated women this way, but she had never experienced it for herself. It was horrible! She had to bow her head when her husband entered the room, speak only with his permission, and this was very little. At times, she forgot what her own voice sounded like. No TV, news, or the Internet. She was lonelier than she could have ever imagined. She was forced to do sexual things that were repulsive to her. She knew that living this way, women from this part of the world would have loved the endless food, money, and the lavish lifestyle. If she was a "good girl," she was treated well. Her life had improved when she learned how she was to behave.

She had a personal attendant who kept her company. They talked and walked in the gardens. There really wasn't a lot she was able to do without any technology. There were parties, and when these happened, she could purchase beautiful gowns. They were unlike anything she had ever seen before. She had a vast array of jewelry to choose from, and the parties always had great music and food. She was once again instructed to stay by his side and not speak unless spoken to. She had been trained what she could and could not say. But since the Dominican Republic, where she found out what had really happened to her, she had become much more observant to the visitors at these parties.

Every month, one of these events would happen, and this would not be for just the businessmen associated in Dubai, but many nationalities. Very wealthy men and women would come and eat, drink, and then be directed to the theater room in the basement of the mansion. Only certain people could partici-pate in this part of the afternoon. She was not privy to this, and in the past, it hadn't mattered, but now she was curious and had a feeling it had to do with the auction. She had noticed that over the past few months, men from different countries would attend. They would come one month alone, then in a couple of months, a woman would accompany them. They were always like Rhonda, the same nationality of the men, submissive, heads down. She had never really noticed before, but extra care was taken to ensure that none of the women got too close to one another. The polite pleasantries could be exchanged, but they were quickly separated if they started to talk too much. Rhonda was able to speak to an Asian lady one time. She looked scared to death, her hands trembling as she held the glass of champagne. The thing that shocked Rhonda the most was her accent. Her husband was Asian and barely spoke a single word of English, and when he did, it was so difficult to understand that he might as well have spoken in his native tongue. But she had a thick Southern accent. The kind you hear when you visit Alabama or a state in the deep South.

After a lot of thought and remembering word for word what had been relayed to her, Rhonda started to fit the pieces together. She needed to see what the men were doing when they went to the basement. Getting there was the problem.

She was kept on a tight leash, and guards were everywhere in the house. Cameras lined every hall and room. Security was so tight, she had no idea how she could possibly pull this off. Then, one day, she had a revelation. It would be risky, and she could be punished severely or killed if it didn't work, but she had to try something.

Her attendant, Ila, had grown close to her over the past few months. She had seemed to have compassion for her when she was punished in the beginning. She had bathed her and helped her soak her sore, beaten body. Once, when she had disrespected her husband and was being punished by fasting for a week, she had smuggled food in to her. Ila was around her age and had dark skin and eyes. She went wherever she wanted to around the house, and no one seemed to notice at all. She dressed in the traditional Eastern Arabia Batula that was common among the women of United Arab Emirates. This tradition typically was only followed by the older women in this area, but Ila continued to follow this. Her face and head were always covered. Rhonda had a great idea, but the problem was if Ila would agree to it.

Rhonda waited until late one night when they were alone. Her husband had been distracted lately; she had no idea what was happening, but he had been agitated and irritable. She had heard yelling, and at one point she could have sworn she heard an American man yelling loudly. Of course, she was always kept at a safe distance, but this was her chance to act because he was very distracted. Ila was bathing her, another issue that made her extremely uncomfortable, to have another woman bathe her, when Rhonda decided to try to talk to her.

"How long have you lived here?" Rhonda asked in an innocent voice.

The silence seemed to last forever, but Ila finally responded by saying, "I came at the same time you came here to live."

"Do you have family?" Rhonda decided to keep pressing on.

Ila explained that she had a mother, father, and brother. Her father had been unable to pay his debt to her husband for a business deal they had made, so she was traded for the payment. What shocked Rhonda so much was that Ila did not seem shocked or sad. Like this was a normal thing to happen. She looked down the entire time she spoke. Not noticeably sad or happy, no emotion crossed her face as she talked. She explained that she liked to be here; the house was beautiful, and she was taken care of. She was never hungry, and she liked to care for Rhonda. Rhonda almost decided to not even attempt the conversation, as she could tell that Ila was happy with her life and may not want to risk changing it. But she pressed on and took the chance.

"Do you know how I came to live here?" she started the conversation. Ila looked at her for a second and shook her head no. "Please let me explain, but this must be a secret between us or I will be severely punished. You don't want that, do you?" Another no, as her eyes remained looking down. Rhonda was drying off and putting on her nightgown. She patted the large bed and motioned for her to sit with her. At first, there was a long hesitation, as Ila was not allowed to sit on the bed, but finally, she submitted and sat. Rhonda told her where she was from and gave her a brief synopsis of the events that led to her coming here. Ila never moved, showed no emotion, and never looked at her. Rhonda went on to tell her that women are being bought and sold and some murdered. Finally, she got the courage to ask if she would help her. She did not want to tell her the plan until she felt she could trust her. Ila quickly stood and picked up the wet towels and dirty linen. She left the room without a word. Rhonda sat with tears starting to stream down her face. Knowing soon she would be beaten, she tried to mentally prepare for what horror was ahead. If Ila told her husband anything she had been told, he would most likely kill Rhonda.

It seemed like forever when she heard the door start to open. Ila walked in with a clothing bag in her hand. She did not look up but said, "Your husband requests to see you in his room within the hour." Rhonda knew what this meant. He would summon her like some type of concubine. Ila would bring in whatever lingerie he wanted her to wear; then she would fix her hair, pick out jewelry, and Rhonda would be sent to his room. Here, she would have to perform whatever sick sexual fantasy he desired. The things that she had been made to do and to endure were depraved and things no woman should have to face. She knew the routine, but it had been a few weeks since she had been called for. Ila never mentioned anything of the conversation; she just helped put on the light-pink lace and leather outfit. The Swarovski crystals that adorned the bra made it sparkle and shine in the candlelight. Her long, black hair was brushed over and over until it shone like glass. It was placed in a soft bun at the nape of her neck. One long comb held it in place. He liked it to be up but then easily pulled down. The hair comb tonight was exquisite. Rhonda was shocked at the elegant accessory for only his eyes, but he was so ostentatious she should not be surprised. The comb was made from diamonds from Africa, Israel, and Russia. Its value was $1,000,000, per Ila.

The walk down the corridor always seemed like the walk of doom to her. It never got easier, no matter how many times it had happened. Ila walked beside her all the way, and then she was expected to wait outside the door and go back to her room with her when he was done with her. Tonight was no different. Rhonda walked into his room. If possible, it was more obnoxiously ornate than the rest of the house. Only a very few were allowed in this room. He was a paranoid man and always thought people were trying to steal from him. But he also did not want people to see what a depraved man he really was.

This particular night, he seemed more anxious than previous nights. He typically just told her what he wanted her to do. At times, he was violent, sometimes more brutal than others, but tonight he was almost tender and loving in the beginning. She was instantly more scared than she had ever been. She knew this was not his nature; he was never like this. Ila had waited outside the door, and she had also noted differences. After Rhonda was in the bedroom, the security guards had accompanied intimidating men down the corridor. There was a door that was well hidden in the corner, and they were discreetly led into the tiny room. Ila stretched her neck to try to see what they were doing. It was a small viewing room; through a mirror, you could see right into the bedroom. This had never happened before. Slowly and carefully, Ila cracked the large door, just a tiny crack that she could see through. The huge mirror that had an enormous frame made of gold was not only a mirror, it was also a window. These men were going to watch the sexual act of Rhonda and her husband. Ila was in shock; she did not recall this ever happening before.

She could see what was happening in the bedroom through the reflection in the mirror. Rhonda also was visibly on edge. She knew he was acting different than he ever had, but she had no idea she was being watched. She knew from the past to not be shy, to do whatever he demanded of her. His new tenderness and affection made her uneasy, but she knew what she had to do to avoid punishment. He started by kissing her, and slowly, as he sat on the top of the bed, he asked her to undress. He sat like a king, his posture arrogant and cocky in between the bedposts. He instructed her what to take off piece by piece. Ila saw that every few minutes, he would glance toward the mirror/window. He then made her stand before him, nude. She was an exquisite woman. Her body perfect in every way, standing there like a trophy or a piece of livestock being sold. She had no idea what was happening, but Ila did. She was nauseated by what she saw. Looking away at multiple times due to being utterly repulsed by what she was witnessing, she tried to put this all in the back recess of her mind. Ila knew getting involved could possibly cost her life. You do not disobey; you do not go against these powerful men because the penalty was often grave. She decided to look one last time, and what she saw this time made her regret the decision. She regretted it because her heart broke for Rhonda. Ila knew what she had to do, no matter what. She had to help her.

CHAPTER 35

Rhonda was exhausted. She had no idea what had just happened. This night was so different than any other. He had been so strange the entire time. He'd had her strip and just stand there while he stared at her; then he told her to do very odd things. She had to walk around the room and then pleasure him in multiple ways. He restrained her at one point, raping her repeatedly, violating her in every way possible. She always tried not to cry out or scream; she refused to give him the satisfaction, but tonight, he was relentless, and she could not take it any longer. The last time he sodomized her, she could not help but cry out. She typically kept her eyes closed, but when she felt something rip deep inside her, she saw him looking at himself in the mirror, a sick smile crossing his arrogant face. He was watching himself rape her over and over. When he saw how exhausted she was and that she was bleeding, he ended the assault. Calling for Ila to come collect her, he went into his shower and never even looked back at her.

Ila helped her from the bed. Knowing that they were being watched and seeing Rhonda's naked abused body, she picked up a throw and covered her. Almost carrying her to the room, she helped her lay on the bed while she ran a hot bath for her. Adding lavender and soothing spices to the water, Ila tried to get a plan together to help her mistress. When she went back into the bedroom and saw her broken and bleeding body on the bed, sympathy welled up within her. She could not help but start to quietly weep for her. Rhonda did not notice; she was like a robot now, taking off her gown and falling into the soothing hot bath. Tears fell over and over, and this was not typical. She always hid her emotions, especially in front of others. But tonight, she was done. She had been pushed to her breaking point. She sat with her eyes closed and seemed to be in a different world. She didn't even seem to notice Ila at all, not until she spoke to her, in a whisper so no one could hear.

"I will help you," she whispered. Rhonda did not seem to hear her at first. She repeated it again and waited.

Finally, after long hesitation, she lifted her head and stared at her. "What made you change your mind?" Her voice was weak and timid as she responded.

"What these men do is wrong and cruel, and I will help you. There have been many American men here the last few weeks, and they seem like something is wrong. Security is different, and they are all angry and anxious. I feel something worse is going to happen, and I fear for you. So, I will help you." This was all Ila said; she did not tell her about the viewing room.

She could tell that this fact may push Rhonda over the proverbial edge.

Nothing else was discussed that night. After putting Rhonda to bed, Ila went to her room in the servants' area of the house. Her mind reviewed the things she had learned and seen with her own eyes over and over all night long. She had to help her; she just did not know how. The nights were always cold and dark, but tonight, the house was darker and colder than she had ever known in her life.

CHAPTER 36

was correct when I thought the agent had unwelcomed news. He was there to tell us there was video footage from the Raleigh airport of a private jet taking off with men that looked like Dr. Ricardo and D. Kepler. Many other men boarded with them. The flight plan and destination that had been given were fake, and at the airport they had reported to land, well, of course, they never arrived. They could have gone anywhere, and we all knew this. I knew the FBI and the international bureaus had been updated. They needed to know how to get Rhonda back. When I asked these questions, Agent Johnson once again had a look of dread across his face. Ishmael had stood up now and looked more intense, if that were even possible.

The agent explained that the relationship between the US and this area of the Middle East was already volatile. The US government did not at this time want to get involved when "some details were speculation."

Immediately, I jumped up, screaming at him, "What do you mean *speculation*?"

He went on to explain that they could not confirm my story that the lady I met was Rhonda. She was dead by all records, and I could be mistaken. They could not risk political unrest to rescue someone they were not certain was even being held against her wishes. The situation had to be handled correctly, and that would take time. The fury on the faces of Ishmael, Ahmed, and me was quite dramatic. Aubrey had started to cry. The emotional stress of the past few weeks was taking a toll on her young psyche. Tears did not enter my eyes; I was not sad or anxious—I was simply furious. I could tell that the agent had no idea what to do or say next. He was as upset as anyone else.

Tripp spoke first, asking, "What do we do now? What comes next?"

Agent Johnson sounded defeated when he explained that they were going through the house and the computers around the clock, trying to get more intel. At this time, locating Kayleigh was the main goal, and the US ambassador would be briefed in a few weeks and contact the accused man in Dubai.

Once again, my voice was loud, rude, and with violent undertones: "Are they stupid or what? If they let him know they're coming, they'll kill her!" I simply could not contain myself. After I ranted and cussed and threw some things, I felt better. When I was finished with my tirade, they just stood there staring at me.

I assumed the agent had all of me he could stand, and he excused himself to leave. Promising to keep us up to date, he left us all to stand there, our minds reeling. Ishmael and Ahmed had been whispering in the corner while we escorted Agent Johnson out. I recognized that look because I had it often. They had a plan; they were going to get Rhonda without the US authorities' help. We all knew the men most likely had left the US, and I was hoping they had taken Kayleigh wherever they had flown to. So, this plan was going to involve me, no matter what. I had Aubrey back, and now I needed Kayleigh.

Ishmael explained that he had wealthy family members there and he could go at any time for a visit. He planned to get a friend's jet and get there as soon as possible and rescue his daughter. I knew we needed to all calm down and try to get a plan together. But I also knew exactly how he felt. I had just felt the same way when I needed to get to my daughter. He was determined; he was boiling from the inside out. Ishmael *had* to find his daughter, and waiting even another moment was torture for him and probably her. He took this very personally. Someone from his own country, his faith, and his "brotherhood" had taken his daughter as a slave. This was a shock to him, and the fact that these men were using the sacred field of medicine to torture innocent women—well, it was too much for his brilliant mind to conceive.

He walked over to me and looked me in the eye. The look he had sent a charge down my spine. "I thank you for what you have done for my daughter. I am going to repay you, but right now, I must get her out of the hell she is in, and I am going to kill the man who has taken my daughter as a slave. I swear to Allah, I will kill this man with my bare hands." His tone was deep and sinister, and I knew with every fiber of my being that he was telling the truth.

Tripp stood across the room staring at me, eyes hard and stern. Ishmael was on the phone, and Aubrey had gone to get some air. I walked over to Tripp and hugged him. This hug was hard and long. I embraced my husband because I missed him and because I was relieved he was not involved. I was ashamed I had even considered that as a possibility. I put my face in the soft part of his neck and took a deep breath. The mix of his body wash and his Polo cologne made me feel safe. This nightmare was far from over, but at that second, in his arms, I was safe and loved. I felt tears fall from his handsome cheeks, and I could not help but get emotional too. But not in an anxious or scared way. A way that felt like relief, like I could feel the end coming.

I stood there and could hear the plans around me going forward. We were all going on this mission. We were all needed to get in, get Rhonda, and look for Kayleigh. We had no way of knowing if she was with them or not, but we had to hope.

CHAPTER 37

Rhonda was exhausted. Physically and mentally, she'd had all she could stand. She had climbed into the hot bath the night before a broken woman, but when Ila whispered in her ear, it was like electricity surged through her. On that particular morning as the sun rose, she sat on her bed and looked out at the Persian Gulf. It was spectacular here. Under normal circumstances, she would have loved the culture and exploring the country, but not like this. The water was blue and clear, not a cloud in the sky. In the distance, she could see the iconic Dubai landmark, the Burj Al Arab. This beautiful sail-shaped building was a tourist attraction and one of the most famous hotels in the world. You could see it billowing high above the sea; only the most distinguished quests frequented this lavish hotel. She had just been allowed to attend one party there, and she had to admit it was a wonderful experience. Yes, she had been treated as a trophy and paraded around the dignitaries like a show pony, but she loved the things she got to see on the short visit there. As much as she would enjoy seeing this part of the world, exploring and learning, she knew that if she ever escaped this, she would never return.

Anxiously awaiting Ila, she dressed and sat on the balcony. Rhonda was so excited when Ila finally arrived with the morning's array of fresh fruit and pastries. She invited her out on the balcony, and they ate together. It would be safer out there, with less chance of their conversation being overheard. Ila started by telling her about the Americans that had been coming. They were staying in various parts of the house. Like she had relayed earlier, there had been some heated arguments between some of them, but she was not sure what about. She did, however, tell Rhonda that a huge party was being planned in two nights. The type where the men came and then went to the "viewing room." She had no idea what this meant, but this would be her chance to find out what was going on.

Ila was being open with Rhonda, so she decided to tell her about her original plan. They could switch places, and if Rhonda put on the traditional attire that Ila wore, in the dim light, it would be difficult to tell them apart. At the previous parties, Rhonda made her appearance and was excused. She sat alone in her room for the remainder of the night. This could work, and as Ila sat quietly, Rhonda could tell she was considering it. After a long pause, Ila agreed that it could work, and they started discussing the details.

Rhonda had hope. She was ecstatic that this might be her way out. Knowledge is power, and if she could find out what was going on, this may help her try to contact someone in the US or even escape. The risks and the chance of death were always in the back of her mind, but she knew she could not live through another night like the past one. She would rather die than remain a slave to the hideous monster she was living with.

She listened intently as Ila tried to tell her everything she could about the layout of the house. She was only allowed in certain areas and was always escorted by security. Ila would have to explain the best she could so no one would be suspicious of her when she was trying to find the viewing room. She tried to explain some of the conversations she had overheard. One American man had arrived with another lady who looked to be American. She had been restrained but appeared to be drugged because she was sleeping. Ila had thought it was odd because she was handcuffed but also asleep. One of the other women attendants had gone and cared for her and washed her. She had told them about her the previous night in the servants' quarters and had been detailed in the extra security measures for her. This concerned Rhonda. She had never seen another female held against her will in the house except for the women who occasionally attended the parties. Why would they bring another American here? Were they going to bring more women to auction? She had to try to save them if this was the case.

They sat on the balcony for hours and walked in the garden that day until they had the plan as close to perfect as they could get. Two nights would be when they made their move, and it could not come soon enough for Rhonda.

CHAPTER 38

The flight from New York to Dubai was close to fourteen hours. I spent most of it dozing, Tripp by my side. Aubrey was sitting with Ahmed, and they were talking every time I looked up. We all had decided to go on the trip after many heated arguments because we all had something we needed. They needed Rhonda back, and I needed Kayleigh. I had no idea if she was there, but I had to try. Also, if the men responsible for this nightmare had sought refuge in Dubai, I wanted to see them, and yes, I wanted to see them punished. We were doing this all on our own with no help from the US government.

Agent Johnson had called my phone over forty-five times by the time we landed. The messages warned over and over not to do anything stupid. They were useless warnings. We all knew this was crazy and extremely risky. Being US citizens going there without the permission of the government, we were asking for trouble, but we had to take the risk.

Ishmael never spoke; he just sat with a stern look on his face, staring out the window. He appeared as volatile as anyone

I had ever seen in my life. Sitting with his fists clenched, lines of stress and fury etched across his face; I could not help to but wonder what was going on in his mind. What was his plan? We could not just walk up to the door and ask to come in. I got up to stretch my legs and decided to talk to him. I did not like the thought of being unprepared and not knowing what was ahead of us.

I went over and looked down at him. I stood there awkwardly and asked if I could be seated. Not speaking, he nodded, and I sat. The silence lasted for quite a few moments, and then I finally asked, "Do we have any idea what we are going to do when we land?"

After another long pause, he informed me that one of his cousins was meeting us at the airport and we were going to his house to decide what our next step would be. He knew we had to go about this carefully or we could all be in danger, especially Rhonda. That was all he said; then he turned to peer out of the window, and I knew the conversation was over. That was all he felt I needed to know and all he was willing to share.

After what seemed like the longest flight possible, we landed and were quickly taken to his family's home. He had already updated the men on what had happened, and they knew who the man was that had taken Rhonda. He lived in a huge mansion in Dubai, and everyone knew of his vast wealth and reputation for being extremely cruel and powerful. They mainly spoke in Arabic, so I understood nothing. The only time we knew what was happening was when he would tell Ahmed what was going on. As luck would have it, there was some type of party at the house the next night. His cousin's wife was a baker and helped in the kitchen. He apparently had many gatherings, and she had been in the house often. Leaving the kitchen was forbidden, but once, she did get to see the dining hall. She thought she remembered seeing Rhonda but had no idea who she was at the time. It seemed to give Ishmael a small amount of peace hearing she was still alive.

We now needed to find a way in. The security was quite impressive, and it would not be an easy task getting in. Determining what type of party would be of great benefit so possibly he could get an invitation. These wealthy men were always having benefit dinners and fundraisers. Maybe this would get him a way in. I decided to walk outside for just a moment to get some air. I had been closed in that plane for so long, and now in this tiny house, I just needed air.

It was hot and dry. No breeze at all, and the temperature was at ninety-six degrees. The sun was high in the sky, and you felt like you were going to bake. The neighborhood where they lived was small, but neat and clean. The "workers" lived in small communities like this one that skirted the elaborate high-rise buildings. I could see them off in the distance. They looked like scary giants looming over a miniature city. The ocean glimmered in the distance. I would have loved to go and spread out a towel and lay in the sun, but this was no vacation; rather, it was a rescue mission. Tripp soon joined me outside and let me know that they had no way to get in. This party was by invitation only, and there was no way to get one. It was very secretive, and no one had any idea what was taking place. So, I had the bright idea of going in as kitchen staff. We could pay off the regular workers and then take their place. That would work! I mean, the only problem was Tripp. If I put on the traditional attire and did not speak, I could go in, and so could Aubrey. The only problem would be not understanding what I was being ordered to do, but it was a risk I could take. Once we went back in the house and discussed it further, we decided this was our only option.

Aubrey, Ahmed, Ishmael, and I planned to go disguised and work in the kitchen. At some point, we would break away and look for Rhonda. The boxes of weapons made me feel nauseated, but I knew in my heart this is what it would come to. Ishmael had sworn to kill the man who did this, and I had no doubt that's just what he would do!

CHAPTER 39

R honda was nervous and excited, and for the first time in a long time, she had hope. She had a wonderful dream while she slept. She had dreamed that her father, a man whom she admired and loved, had come to rescue her. She knew in her heart this was impossible, but the dream had felt so real. She had awakened refreshed and with hope. Ila was nervous too. She wanted to help, but she was afraid for both of their lives. The day was spent decorating the house and getting the expensive foods and final preparations ready. Ila explained to Rhonda she had never seen the master of the house go to such extravagant lengths for any other parties. They had spared no expense with the most expensive champagne and foods flown in from all over the globe.

The dress was the most gorgeous one yet—simply breath-taking. Rhonda knew he was trying to impress someone to go to this expense. The dress was couture from a famous designer in Dubai named Rami Al Ali. She could not help but feel beautiful and sexy in the magnificent dress. Her husband's personal

assistant had told Ila to make sure she looked her "most beautiful" tonight. Ila had tried to pry to see what was going on but
was quickly dismissed. You could almost feel the electricity in
the room. Getting ready in the gorgeous gown and the excitement of the mission they were about to undertake had Rhonda's
adrenaline at a high. She replayed the events over and over in
her mind. They would go to the dinner as always; she would be
the obedient wife, smile, and keep her eyes down and lips closed.
When she was dismissed, she would come back with Ila, and she
would put on her attire. This would allow her to move more
freely in the house, and Ila would lay in the bed and appear to
be sleeping in case someone decided to check on her.

The room was decorated unlike anything she had ever
seen. The food and champagne were in unlimited supply.
Fancy pastries and cocktails served on silver trays were offered to the guests, and what a gathering it was. She had never seen such intimidating men in her entire life. They were
wealthy, powerful men, once again of all ethnicities. She also
noticed some guests had translators, and some did not. But
what was the most interesting was the American men that
had joined them. This was not normally the case, so she was
shocked. Trying not to stare and look suspicious, she peered
at the American man a little too long and was quickly reminded to put her eyes down. She was not to make direct eye
contact with any male, ever. This had been the cause of many
beatings when she first arrived.

It seemed as if everyone was on edge. She could not tell
if it was excitement due to the party or if it was just in her

imagination. The party was longer than usual, and once again, Rhonda could not help but to notice how over the top her husband seemed tonight. Finally, she was dismissed, but she had felt that she was being watched all night. Was she paranoid? At one point, she even felt like the kitchen staff had been staring at her. She was about to panic, thinking that her husband was on to her and was having everyone keep an eye on her when she was finally escorted to her room. Ila followed, and the true excitement started!

Adorned in the traditional attire of a female in that country, Rhonda was able to walk freely. It felt amazing to her since in the past she had been privy to very little of the house. Her heart was pounding in her chest and head. She was terrified but excited all at the same time. She passed many people in the hallways, all servants rushing in and out, attending to the needs of the guests. Soon, the other women were excused, and like before, the men were taken down to a viewing room. Ila's instruction had worked well with helping her navigate herself, and she was able to get ahead of the group of men, hiding herself up in the loft of the room. The theater room had rows of leather chairs that faced a huge movie screen. The ornate stained-glass windows lined the top edge of the room. She was able to slide in and lay flat, looking into the room through a small crack. The men all had glasses of expensive scotch or other after-dinner cocktails, laughing and talking as they entered the room. Finally, after a lot of banter, an Arabic man stood to speak. He was joined by an American man who stood beside him.

Rhonda did not know either and was puzzled when her husband was not taking the lead. The man welcomed the group and explained they would be discussing the business at hand shortly. He introduced the American visitor as Dr. Ricardo. He had graciously joined them from the USA to discuss what he had to offer.

Rhonda had heard most of what he said before, in the Dominican. Dr. Ricardo discussed the auction and how successful it had been. He explained how since so many different women come to the US, it is easy for the men to request what type of women they desire. So many different nationalities come to the US and are born there; no matter where you are from, they can match you with the perfect woman. He went into detail about how the woman is declared dead, so there is no way to trace them—no one comes to look for them. The method is discreet and virtually foolproof. Of course, the men are welcome to go to the next body auction, but their specific needs may not be met. All the men had to do was explain what they desired and pay the initial fee, and a match would be found.

At this point in the presentation, Rhonda's husband stood and interjected. He explained that was how he was able to purchase Rhonda. "I explained that I wanted a pure woman of Egyptian descent. Beautiful, intelligent, and with no ties. I did not want to deal with family issues, etc., so this option was perfect for me. I was relieved that she was not able to be traced and I did not have to worry about her ever being located. Yes, she was difficult to train at first, but she has been trained now, and as you all witnessed the other night, she will do whatever I tell her to do. I have broken her to my will like a trained stallion."

Rhonda had no idea what he meant, but a sick feeling consumed her as she remembered the night he'd been so strange. She could not allow herself to get emotional now; she had to remember the task at hand and focus. The lights were dimmed, and a film started. It was a film that started by showing the flag of the USA. It was blowing in the wind, and for a moment, she felt like crying. She missed America—the freedom and the culture. She had taken for granted that not all countries allow women to be free and independent. Then the faces of powerful women went across the screen, multiple rich women in business and politics. In the background, the narrator explained how women in the USA "did not know their place; some even think they can be president! Women have no right ruling over men, and this is a way for you men to put the American woman back where they belong. You can purchase almost any American woman you choose, and in secrecy, she will belong to you—be a slave to you in every way." The man went on the explain how the women were told that if they ever tried to escape, the families and people they loved would die. "Woman are so protective and ignorant, they don't try to escape and submit to their new lives easily. You see, women are less than men; they were created to serve man, not be equal. They are ignorant and easily broken, and if you aren't happy with the purchase, you can sell her back for resale or dispose of her yourself."

Rhonda swallowed back the bile that had gathered in her throat. They were discussing American woman like they were cattle at a sale. Individual men stood and gave personal testimonials of the wives they had purchased and how well it had gone for them. These were the men Rhonda had seen women with at previous parties. They also explained that they could purchase more than one woman, and once again, they could always attend an auction. Some of the men wanted a woman of their ethnic background to bear children but wanted the true typical American woman to have as a concubine. This was discussed in detail also.

The presentation seemed to go on and on with a question and answer session. One man asked Dr. Ricardo if he could be trusted—after all, he was American. His answer shocked Rhonda. He said, "I feel like a woman's place is by her husband's side, and in the USA, it is out of control. The women have no respect for men, and when one almost became president, well, that was enough for me. This auction will not change the course of women in that country, but it makes some men feel better and more powerful, and I make money doing it!" With that, he raised his glass, and the men laughed and cheered.

They discussed that no women were ever taken from their country of origin, and none would ever be. If a woman was taken outside the US, she was an American that had moved there or was visiting. They had contacts all over the globe, so the possibilities were endless. At that moment, Rhonda almost started to cry. She knew she could not beat these men and save herself, let alone anyone else. These psychopaths were out of control, and she was not sure how she ever thought she could save herself. Quietly, she got out of her little hiding spot and started to make her way back to her room. She had her head and eyes down and was hoping the tears that were streaming could not be seen. She had been so distraught she had not noticed she was being followed and never saw the man grab her from behind.

CHAPTER 40

Ila lay still in the bed, frozen, paranoid that someone would come in. She could hardly breathe when the door slowly opened. It was dark; they would think she was asleep and leave. But when she heard footsteps coming toward her, she was about to panic when she heard a low male voice. "Rhonda? Is that you?" Ila turned to look and saw who appeared to be a kitchen servant looking at her over the side of the bed. The man looked shocked when he saw Ila instead of Rhonda. She sat up and started to beg immediately for her life. He held his hands up in front of himself as a sign of peace and explained he would not hurt her. She knew he was American and felt relieved to some degree.

After a few intense moments, he explained that he was Rhonda's brother and he was there to rescue her. He wanted to know where she was, and Ila started to quickly explain. She tried to wrap all she could up in the short amount of time she had. Ahmed was flabbergasted that Rhonda was trying to escape on her own and was worried; this would be much more difficult. He relayed to Ila that he had some people with him to help and wanted to know how long Rhonda would be gone. They decided he would go back to the kitchen and let the others know what was going on. Ila felt it would be safer to try to get Rhonda out when the guests were gone. The extra security made it much riskier to do anything, but later in the night, this would decrease significantly. Ahmed agreed and swore to Ila he would return soon. He quietly left the room, and when the door opened in only a few moments, Ila thought he had come back early. She was shocked to see it was Rhonda returning.

She was scared and anxious before Ila could even speak. Rhonda explained that a man had grabbed her and told her to go straight to her room and tell Rhonda how she was going to be rescued. The man had thought she was really Ila and was sending Rhonda a message. This was when Ila told her about her visit from Ahmed. Rhonda could not believe her brother was there. He was in the house to save her! Then fear gripped her. If he were caught, they would kill him. He was her brother, and she could not let him die. Ila saw her fear and tried to comfort her. He had promised he had help and he would be back; all they could do was wait.

Time seemed to move at the pace of a turtle. Rhonda paced the floor for what seemed like hours. She and Ila had seen most of the men and the security leave a few hours ago and could not understand why nothing had happened yet. Finally, when a light knock came on the door, she could not get it opened fast enough. When she opened it, she could not believe what she saw.

I was standing there in my Arabic garb, and when I pulled the face cloth down, the shock crossed her face. She pulled me into the door and embraced me hard and long. "What are you doing here? Where is my brother? What is going on?"

The anxiety and worry were written across her face. I was still shocked at how beautiful she was. I quickly explained how we had gotten in and as the kitchen staff was being dismissed for the night, I was able to get away to her. Ahmed and Ishmael, along with the other men, had gone to look for her husband. She was shocked and stood in disbelief when I told her that her father had come. She was relieved, scared, and worried all at the same time. I explained that we all needed to get dressed and try to get out with the servant women leaving. Ila was not a fan of our plan, but we had to try to get out. I knew it was a matter of time before things got ugly. There was a food truck out back waiting for us. As I helped Rhonda get changed, Ila went to check the hallways for security. When she returned and let us know it was safe, we quietly went down the long corridor. Suddenly, there were popping sounds all around us. In shock at first, I didn't realize it was gunfire. Two large men came running toward us, and we were all three taken into another room. The guns seemed huge to me, and the men seemed like something out of a movie. I felt like I was in a movie, the never-ending horror film. I could not understand a word they were yelling, but the earpieces were where their orders were coming from. Rhonda and Ila were tied, and when the man came to me and pulled down my face covering, he was clearly shocked I was American. Yelling loudly into his mouthpiece while he restrained me, I caught a glimpse of Ila's expression. I had no idea what he said, but by the look on her face, it wasn't good.

Soon, Rhonda's husband and a few more men arrived. He walked straight over to her and backhanded her so hard she fell to the floor. She quickly sat back up straight, proud and ready for more. This infuriated him even more, and he drew his hand back for another strike when the door opened again. To my great surprise, in walked my old friend, Dr. Ricardo. I just sat there, my mouth hanging open, wanting to say so much but at this moment lost for words.

He walked calmly over to me and laughed. "Layla, my dear, it sure took you long enough to figure this out, didn't it? Bless your heart, as you Southerners say!" He was laughing almost hysterically in my face. My first instinct happened before I even knew it as I spat in his face. I met the same punishment as Rhonda with a sharp backhand to the face. I had not even noticed one of the security guards until he walked over to us. He pulled out a small gun, and before Rhonda could do anything, he shot Ila in the head. Not a word, not a sound—he just shot her. Rhonda screamed in agony. Tears started to pour, and I was once again in such shock that I just sat there. He then walked over to me, gun ready, pointed at my head. Dr. Ricardo stood back with a sickening smile; I knew I needed to stall them. Help was on the way. They were here in the house; we just needed to give them time to find us.

"Wait, wait, can I just ask you something before I die? "He smiled and motioned for the man to wait on my execution. "I just want to know why you, as a healer, a physician, would do this? Why would you kill Kayleigh? She loved you, did you know that? You are a loved man and a great doctor; why would you do these insane things you have done?"

"You, my dear, of all people should know how I like to live; you saw my home. I am a businessman. Medicine only takes from us. We get paid to kill ourselves taking care of rude patients. They are ungrateful, mean, and they never appreciate what we do for them. They yell at us, cuss us, and never consider what we do for them. People have become so ungrateful, and now with the government, we make less and get sued more often. I stopped caring about the patients years ago. I need to take care of myself. To do that, I joined in the business of the auction, and it has been quite amazing for me. I know Kayleigh loved me, and you have no business bringing her up, so unless you have anything else to say, it is time for you to die. You have caused me nothing but trouble since the beginning."

I could tell I struck a sore spot with the mention of Kayleigh; I think he cared for her. So, I dug in. "She had never felt that way about anyone; she would have done anything for you, but you betrayed her. What did you do? Kill her? Sell her? Let someone harvest her organs? You are an animal, and I hope you meet the same fate as those women you have tortured! What about Whitley? Do you remember her? She was a beautiful light, and you snuffed her out in her youth?" I knew I needed to try to keep my word to Krissy, so I decided to keep digging.

After another nice hit to the face, my ears ringing, he started to talk again. He was furious, red-faced, and volatile. "I told you to shut your mouth about Kayleigh, or I swear, I will kill you myself, and it will not be as painless as a bullet to the head. I do remember Whitley. Yes, she was an amazing young lady. She made me a fortune, with her rare blood type. When the emperor of an Asian country called—his daughter needed a heart-lung transplant—well, she was perfect. She made me more than an entire auction with that harvest!"

The vomit spewed from me before I even felt it coming. They took her organs while she was alive. I was in hell! I just sat there, vomit hanging from my mouth, sweat pouring off my head, defeated. Rhonda's head was down; she was weeping, with blood splatter all over her and brain matter from her friend Ila covering her clothing. The gun barrel felt cool to my hot forehead; I was waiting to hear the pop and wondered if I would hear it and feel it at the same time. When I heard the loud pop, I thought, *Hey, that wasn't too bad. I mean, it was loud, but I didn't have any pain.* I felt blood pouring down my face, but I didn't fall over yet. Then I heard Rhonda scream and opened my eyes. Realizing I was not the one shot and the blood I felt was not mine was a relief. Shouting and guns, blood splattered all over. Ishmael and Ahmed had come in with guns blazing. They shot whoever they thought was to blame and had no mercy. I was still sitting, tied, staring, and in shock with Rhonda beside me. She had never seen her father kill and definitely not her baby brother.

Time seemed to stop when Ishmael had Rhonda's husband up against the wall. He had been hit, but it was only a flesh wound. They were speaking in Arabic, and I had no idea what they were saying, but it could not have been good. He had him by the neck, off the ground, and in front of us all, he wrapped his hands around his neck and squeezed the life out of him. Ahmed had Dr. Ricardo in the corner, and when he tried to fight and run, he was shot before he even got to the door. It seemed I was sitting in a sea of dead bodies.

I was able to hold myself together better than Rhonda. She was hysterical at this point. Ishmael came over and picked her up, and Ahmed untied us. We needed to get out of the house before others came. We were placed in a truck and quickly taken out of the city. For some reason, I did not feel closure. I knew that there were more women out there, I knew I had to go home and tell Krissy about Whitley. At this point, all I wanted to do was to wash the blood and innards off me. The amount of brain and blood all over me was grotesque.

Seeing Tripp and Aubrey made me feel better, but all I wanted to do was to go home. I needed to be home; I desperately needed for this to be over, really over. But I knew it wasn't—not yet.

CHAPTER 41

We had to wait a few hours before we could board the plane, so I took a walk. The ocean was the most beautiful blue I had ever seen and crystal clear. The sea was calm, no choppy waves, no storms on the horizon. I walked down to the water and put my feet and legs in. As I looked out over the ocean, I remembered back to the start of this story. I thought when I woke up in that coffin I had survived; I had cheated death and was going to live. But I was wrong—I did die that night. The old Layla was dead. The person I was then, standing in the water, was not the same woman placed in that coffin. The person I was walking out of that sea as was different in many ways. I was not timid; I did not fear death. I was braver, stronger, and no longer naïve. Evil was rampant in this world. I had always known that, but it had not touched my life in my little Southern town.

As I stared into the water, I thought of the wonders of nature. How God in his infinite wisdom created this earth and the creatures on it so brilliantly. He had answered my prayers, and my family was safe.

I remembered reading about the mimic octopus, a very special animal. It not only can change colors to adapt to its surroundings, but it also can change its appearance if needed. It can look like various animals in the sea, such as a sea snake, jellyfish, etc. They burrow themselves on the sea floor to not be seen, and they blend in. This was what those physicians had done. They had infiltrated the medical field, and their poison tentacles had reached around the globe. They blended in, and no one suspected what they were doing. There would be no way to find all the women they had sold. No way to know the number of women harvested for their organs.

I could not go back to practicing medicine as a nurse practitioner. I had to help and make a difference. If Kayleigh was able to be an RN and FBI agent, I could help even more being a provider. I could go places and do things she could not. I may be able to find more of these crazy men. Even if I could save one woman, I had to try. I discussed my plan with Aubrey, and she understood. Tripp, however, was a different story. But he knew he had lost his previous wife, and this was what was left of her. Changes would be made as soon as we got back to the USA. I was nervous, excited, and anxious about my choice. But oddly, not scared. I think that emotion was one I had put in the back of my subconscious, and I intended to keep it there. My first mission was to find Kayleigh. I knew she was out there, somewhere.

CHAPTER 42

Darkness, hunger, cold, so cold. Kayleigh had no idea how many days it had been since she had eaten and heard a voice from outside. Her new owner had promised he would return but had not, and she had no idea where she was. She felt like time marched slowly. The fear of the unknown was the worst; not knowing what they planned to do with her was going to kill her faster than starvation. Something had happened many nights ago; she had heard gunfire over and over. She awaited rescue, but no one came.

Right when she was about to fall asleep again, the door of the small room opened. Taking a few moments for her eyes to adjust wasn't long enough. Because the person standing in front of her was not at all who she expected and reminded her all over her the torture was just starting for her. . . .

CPSIA information can be obtained
at www.ICGtesting.com
Printed in the USA
LVHW020658010719
622841LV00022B/1203